Straight Beast Mode 2

Straight Beast Mode 2

Lock Down Publications & Ca$h
Presents
STRAIGHT BEAST MODE 2
A Novel by *De'Kari*

Straight Beast Mode 2

Lock Down Publications
P.O. Box 944
Stockbridge, Ga 30281

Visit our website at www.lockdownpublications.com

Copyright 2022 by De'Kari
Straight Beast Mode 2

All rights reserved. No part of this book may be reproduced in any form or by electronic or mechanical means, including information storage and retrieval systems without permission in writing from the publisher, except by a reviewer who may quote brief passages in review.
First Edition June 2022
Printed in the United States of America

This is a work of fiction. Names, characters, places, and incidents either are products of the author's imagination or are used fictitiously. Any similarity to actual events or locales or persons, living or dead, is entirely coincidental.

Book interior design by: **Shawn Walker**
Edited by: **Tamira Butler**

Stay Connected with Us!

Text **LOCKDOWN** to 22828 to stay up-to-date with new releases, sneak peaks, contests and more…

Submission Guideline

Submit the first three chapters of your completed manuscript to ldpsubmissions@gmail.com, subject line: Your book's title. The manuscript must be in a .doc file and sent as an attachment. Document should be in Times New Roman, double spaced and in size 12 font. Also, provide your synopsis and full contact information. If sending multiple submissions, they must each be in a separate email.

Have a story but no way to send it electronically? You can still submit to LDP/Ca$h Presents. Send in the first three chapters, written or typed, of your completed manuscript to:

LDP: Submissions Dept
P.O. Box 944
Stockbridge, Ga 30281

*DO NOT send original manuscript. Must be a duplicate. *

Provide your synopsis and a cover letter containing your full contact information.

Thanks for considering LDP and Ca$h Presents.

De'Kari

Acknowledgments

From C1ty:

First off, I would like to give all praise to Allah. I thank my brother, the writer of this book, for letting me be in the book and using my input on it. I would also like to thank my grandma SJ, my kids: Jojo, Zachariah, and Jeremiah; my brothers: Cieno, Wes, and Dell; my sister DQ, my cousins: Rio, Eric, Will aka XO, DJ, etc... lol. My right hand, CJ, and finally, Genesis and Danny Perez. Thanks for all the love and support.

From Lil' Dooka:

First and foremost, I want to thank God for giving me the time, strength, and patience to work with my big brother De'Kari in creating this book. Second, I would like to thank my mom. She's my backbone, best friend, helping hand. It's unconditional, Mama! But you already know that, Carrie Manuel, lol. Love you, Mama.

I would like to thank all of my family, brothers, sisters, nephews, my little nieces, and everyone else that makes up my support system. Laura, Megan, GM Jean Whitney, Malik, Uncle Dame Jack (Omega), GM Sherrie, Auntie Marsha, Oscar, Corey, Harold (eoro), Erica, Pauline (TBW), Emily, Ali, Liz, Big Ree, P-Smacks, Lamar, Jessica, Bob, Brittany, Legend, Mason, Dre Mare, Wa'Lae Torri, Angeli, Kevyn money, Chop 064, Boo 4, Rich 4, Tay 4ever Greezy, Turk Geez, Tana Gunz, Moguttah, Tommy, Bubz, 4-Boy, Budda, Sace, T4, Domo, Philthy, Nino 4, Greez, Chink, Reco, Waka, Mari, Lil' Tone 52, Lil' D-boy, Bobby, LILLAR, Baam, BC Cozy, Juice, Rich 10, Nard, Dex Krueger, Pooh 42, Brevin, Salute Muk, Tyrizzle, Koala, Nae, Tae Happy, Boo, Auntie Lib, Auntie Nell, Auntie D, Auntie Lee, Auntie Nina, Auntie V, Grandma Vai, Cisco, Carl, Kam, KMari, Mill, Briella, Baby Turk, Baby Mali, Baby Wap, Tia 3400, Nay 3400, Mookie, Milli Millz, MiMi MeMe, Paige, Lil' Ant

Straight Beast Mode 2

34, Bella, CiCi, TeTe, CeCe, Baby Stevie, D-Lo (Menlo Park), Weezy 25 (EPA Village), L's (EPA), T.A.G. TC, Lil' Junior (EPA), Vic (EPA), TuTu.

A Four to all my Fallen. "I Love Y'all: LL B.R., LL 2X, LL Sai, LL Vontae, LL Nito, LL Tee, LL Jaden 52, LL Meek, LLRT, LL Daba."

#ForeverGreezy #SAIwrld #Vontaeville #NitoLord #TeeBlock #JordanPark #DSammy #CMB-Meek #Hithard-RT #4evaDaDaWinnin #TIO #YT #LPD #LLKclap #LL-Eddie #LL-Yose #M&M #Flyhigh

De'Kari

Straight Beast Mode 2

"Over My Body"
By: Dook Bang

The Devil took over my body, swear dese niggaz bet not try me. Bitch, I'm thugging to the death, and all my niggaz right beside me. The Devil took over my body. Swear dese niggaz bet not try me. Bitch, I'm thugging to the death, and all my niggaz right beside me.
    And I do it for BR, nigga.... Think you tough? I'll guarantee I'll pull your card, nigga....
    They took BR. They took Sai and Vontae in the same year. I was sitting in that cell. Damn near dropped a million tears. All a nigga did was cry, I couldn't even slide. I swear I ain't believe it when they said you niggaz died. They asking me if I'm alright, they see the pain in my eyes. I'm still asking God why he took my niggaz out my life. Took my energy to try like I ain't even wanna rap no more. The bitch that set up Yase, nigga we gone smack that hoe. They say the energy you give, then that's what you gone receive. Bitch, I stand on my decision made a vow to never leave. I'mma slide for my brother, till the day I go to sleep. Don't do it for myself, I do it for Baby Greezy.
    The Devil took over my body. Swear dese niggaz bet not try me. Bitch, I'm thugging to the death, and all my niggaz right beside me.
    And I do it for BR nigga....
    Tear It Off Dook

De'Kari

Prologue

MoMo stood up from the couch to go answer the loud banging on the door. He figured it was Lil' Dooka and the rest of the TIO Click. His band of brothers. It was time for MoMo to finally come clean with the secret of his betrayal.

As he made his way to the door TG's words played in his mind. "Don't even sweat that shit, brodie. We gonna fix this shit and push on like we always do! Nigga, it's 4Ever Greezy!"

MoMo paused just before he reached the front door and looked over his shoulder at TG sitting on the couch. "4Ever Greezy!" he repeated before turning to open the front door of Auntie Dee's apartment.

He opened the front door, and all of the color drained from his face. MoMo looked like he had seen a ghost.

"Nigga, fuck TIO and fuck Tre-4!" MoMo was staring directly at none other than C1ty himself.

C1ty was standing roughly five feet back from the entrance to Auntie Dee's apartment. He was dressed in black jeans and boots, with an all-black hoodie on. The hood was down, exposing C1ty's entire head and face. His long, black Lord Jesus dreadlocks hung over his shoulders and down his back, loose and wild like the mane of a lion. In his hands was an all-black, pistol grip, sawed-off Mossberg pump. To MoMo, C1ty looked scarier than the Grim Reaper himself.

The moment C1ty knew he had MoMo's attention, he squeezed the trigger. MoMo never had the opportunity to react. The blast caught him in his abdomen and chest. The force of the blast lifted MoMo off his feet, knocking him backward five feet into the apartment....

De'Kari

Chapter 1

TG was placing his Glock 20 on his waist when the sound of the Mossberg erupted, disturbing the peace and quiet that had settled over the inside of the apartment. He turned his head toward the sound of the blast in time to see MoMo knocked off his feet. It was nothing like the movies nor the shit niggaz read in the pages of them urban books. Shit didn't slow down in real life. Instead, it felt like everything sped up.

As MoMo's body hit the ground, TG was already on his feet lifting his banger. His first two shots flew wildly. TG wasn't worried about that. Those shots were only intended to let whoever was shooting know that they had some resistance. Let them know that wasn't shit sweet around this bitch!

C1ty was marching into the apartment ready to murk shit when TG started to return fire. C1ty ducked back into the depths of the hallway so fast that he stumbled into Murda, who was down on one knee aiming his Glock 27 at the doorway, desperately trying to get off a shot. Just as he made out the form of a body, C1ty stumbled into him. More shots rang out coming from inside the apartment. Murda scrambled away from C1ty. As soon as he was clear, Murda squeezed off two shots of his own. His objective was to ensure whoever the shooter was in the house, they didn't advance and catch them sleeping.

A bullet flew past Murda only a few inches from the left side of his head. Most niggaz would have ducked low or at least flinched. You don't get a name like Murda without being tried and proven. He was too seasoned to flinch. This usually gave Murda the upper hand in situations like this, and today was no different. By standing his ground, he was able to spot TG as he came up from behind an overturned table. TG thought Murda would duck down from the last shots he sent at him. This miscalculation cost him dearly.

Murda squeezed the trigger in rapid succession. Four 40-caliber missiles tore through the air. The first three barreled into TG's chest, hell bent on causing destruction. TG stumbled backward. This was his first time ever being shot. The shots hurt like a mothafucka! Like somebody stuck three burning hot steel rods into his chest. He couldn't focus on the pain. He had to bust back because he refused to let the sucka side take him. He raised his arm to send some hot shit their way, but he never got the chance. Murda, once seeing that he had hit his target, rose to his feet and relentlessly kept firing.

TG jerked backward as another missile tore into the front of his left shoulder. It was then that TG knew it was over. The only thought in his mind was niggaz would forever say that he let the sucka side penetrate their turf and catch him slipping.

Murda took a step to advance, and C1ty was right behind him. They both could smell the allure of the kill right at their fingertips. Eager, they moved in for the kill. Gunfire erupted from their left, interrupting their murderous plans. Stopping at the sound of the new gunfire in their gunfight saved Murda's life. Had he have taken his next step, his brains would have landed on C1ty's shoulder. Instincts made Murda and C1ty spin. Once again, C1ty dropped to one knee and brought the Mossberg up.

Lil' Nardy was the first to round the corner. He, Turk, and Reco were all at Cement Hill drinking and smoking when the shooting first started. Reco was the first to react but at 6'1" and 147 lbs, Lil' Nardy was the fastest out the click, so he got to the corner first. Nardy was holding a Glock 29 in his hands, and he was letting that mothafucka get off!

C1ty opened up the Mossberg. The mighty boom it made as he kept his finger on the trigger and repeatedly jacked the pump off woke up the entire neighborhood. Nardy ducked back behind the building. The sound of the Mossberg put the fear of God in the young soldier. By then, Turk and Reco made it to where Nardy was standing.

"Nigga, what the fuck is going on?" Reco asked Nardy as he gripped the Glock 30 in his hands.

"Them bitch-ass 357 niggaz! I think they got TG and MoMo trapped inside of Auntie Dee's." When he heard this, Reco snuck a peek around the corner. When he did that, Murda squeezed his trigger, sending shots at Reco. Trying to knock his mothafuck'n head

Straight Beast Mode 2

off. Reco quickly ducked back behind the building to avoid the shots. Murda used the time to quickly slap in a new clip.

"Nigga, we ain't about to sit here and let them fuck niggaz have us stuck hiding behind the building like we spooked. Like shit is sweet round this bitch. You niggaz get ready. When I count to three, we just gonna bend the corner and give these niggaz the business. It is what it is, nigga, they can't hit us all." Turk was tired of these 357 bitches.

Neither Nardy nor Reco said a word in response. They just waited for the countdown. When Turk got to three, they all stepped from behind the building, guns ready to blaze. If only there was someone there to shoot at. C1ty and Murda were nowhere in sight. Together they ran to Auntie Dee's. None of them were ready for the sight they saw. MoMo was on the ground a few feet inside of the apartment. The entire front side of his shirt was soaked in blood. MoMo was moaning while squirming on the floor. Blood was all over the floor around him.

Reco stepped past Nardy and walked into the apartment. MoMo looked fucked up, and Reco didn't think he was going to make it. From the sound of the sirens the police were close. There was so much gun smoke in the air, the sulfur was burning Reco's eyes as he searched for TG. He finally spotted TG on the ground behind an overturned table. Reco didn't think TG looked as bad as MoMo, but he was pretty fucked up too!

"Fuck!" Reco yelled out of anger and frustration. He was tired of seeing his team take losses.

"Brah, we gotta get out of here!" Turk called from the porch. He didn't get any closer because he didn't want to see his brothers all fucked up. Laid out on the floor all shot the fuck up.

"Nigga, we 'posed to just leave these niggaz like this?" Reco spun around with death in his eyes.

"Reco, brah, we can't do shit for 'em if them pigs came up in here and we got these fucking guns on us!" Turk didn't want to leave either, but the rules of the game were what they were. The rules said they had to get the fuck out of there.

De'Kari

"Turk's right, Reco. We gotta go hood. On BR, I don't wanna leave, but we gotta go." Nardy was almost on the verge of tears, but he held them bitches in.

The sound of the sirens became dangerously close. Reco hated it with a passion, but that didn't stop the shit from being true. If they didn't leave, they would no doubt end up at 850 Bryant St. getting booked into jail. Reco felt like he was turning his back on MoMo and TG as he ran out of the apartment and away from the projects with Nardy and Turk. Their destination... Cement Hill.

***

Budda had just gotten off of the phone with his little bitch, Ariane. The news she had given him had Budda beyond pissed off and grief stricken. It seemed like all of his little niggaz were dropping like flies. When the beef first started Budda was against it because it was all over a bitch. Yet once the bullets started flying and Bubbz got it, it was too late to fall back. Them 357 niggaz shooting up Bubbz's funeral and killing his mom turned the beef into a war.

Budda left the yard and walked across the dayroom. His long hair tied into a single thick braid swung like a dragon's tail down his back in between his shoulder blades. As he marched across the dayroom of 4-West in his orange pants and orange V-neck with San Mateo County Jail logo stamped on them, he knew it was time. He had to get his mind ready because of the decision he just made.

He walked up to the little Filipino kid that was sitting on a chair typing away on a tablet doing legal work. "What's up, nigga?" Budda spoke. When the kid looked up Budda told him, "I need you to hook me up real quick."

"What you need?" The kid's name was JR. He was from the Low. The Low and 4 had their own little beef going on, but they left that street shit in the streets.

JR was a real beast when it came to that legal shit. Yet he was even more of an animal when it came to braiding hair.

"Take me to the streets."

"Damn, so it's time? I was wondering how long it was going to take before your ass had enough of this bullshit." JR logged out of the tablet and stood up.

"I just got off the phone with my bitch. She told me them niggaz just shot up Auntie Dee's spot. MoMo and TG was up in there. Both of them little niggaz got hit bad. What kind of nigga would I be to sit back and keep watching from the sidelines while my little niggaz losing?"

"The 357 niggaz done fucked up now." JR walked to his bathroom to grab his hair grease and combs.

Budda had been in San Mateo County for almost two years fighting two attempted murders, three great bodily injuries, and a few reckless mayhems. His bail was five million dollars. He didn't remain in the county because he didn't have the money. Posting the bail would set off all types of red flags. Because of that, he had said fuck bailing out. He would fight his case from behind the wall.

Enough was enough. Budda had to finally say fuck raising alarms behind posting bail. His niggaz needed him, and he wasn't about to let them down. It was TIO till the death, and Budda wasn't dead yet.

JR made it back to the table that Budda had sat at. He talked to Budda as he began braiding his hair, but Budda was lost in his own thoughts.

Budda been 'bout that life ever since a young nigga. He bust his first gun at thirteen. It wasn't in the air or at no fucking beer bottles. It was at a fuck nigga that wouldn't Tear It Off. His pistol play was immaculate, and his body count was proof of his lethal appetite for destruction. This was long before any of the beefs started. The beef only made him worst. Standing 6'0", Budda only weighed about 150 pounds when he first fell. That was before he got on "That Body by Voorheeze" workout the entire jail was doing.

Voorheeze was this legendary BGF nigga that had helped establish a branch of the organization called Neva Die Dragon Gang. He was a beast in the field. He and his team became legends after they declared war on the police. While he was in jail and prison, Voorheeze had his own style of working out. His unique style put

80 pounds of muscle on the Dragon Gang General and was adopted by nearly every nigga that had the heart to push their bodies to the limit.

Budda was one of them niggaz. He was now 205 pounds of fierce muscle. He was a unique mixture of Chinese, Filipino, and Black, with some Samoan in there. None of that mattered or stayed on a nigga's mind when they saw Budda. His eyes were the only thing that jumped out at niggaz. They were a dull, flat gray like the tombstone of a cemetery. There was no spark of life inside of those eyes. Only death. Times like now, when he was angered, was the only time electricity was in those eyes. Then and only then. When angered, the gray of his eyes resembled the gray storm clouds in the sky. Radiated by the electricity of lightning.

A storm was coming to Sunnydale, alright. But instead of water, this storm was going to rain bullets.

Chapter 2

Trucho and Casper sat in the living room playing *Fortnite* on PS4. They were on the Battle Royal mode. Casper had been trying to hide from the funk, but the storm was forcing him ever so close to the actual action. Trucho, on the other hand, was bringing it to the other players. Battle Royal mode was every man for himself. One hundred players all trying to kill each other to see who would be the last man standing. It was a video game version of *The Purge*.

"Yeah, fool, the storms forcing that ass to have to come and get some. That ass can't keep running from the funk," Trucho teased Casper, as his character snuck up on an unsuspecting character that was trying to find some treasure inside of an empty house. Trucho's character killed the unsuspecting fool, and Trucho stood up and did the Millie Rock.

"See that, homeboy? That's how you knock some shit down!" Trucho gloated as he waved his arms.

Casper wasn't worried about Trucho or his showboating. Casper knew he was 'bout that life. He was just letting Trucho's dumb ass take all the risk getting rid of all Casper's light weight for him. Then Casper would pop up and pop off! Unfortunately, that wasn't going to be today.

A loud whistle pierced through the air, making its way inside of the house and to their ears. It was a call from one of the little homies that were posted as lookouts on the block. The call meant something was going down. Mothafuckas had to get ready. Trucho paused the game. He and Casper both reached for their guns just as Smokey came into the front door.

"We got about nine, ten cars rolling hard down the block!" Smokey didn't come all the way into the house. He stuck his head and upper part of his body in the door.

After giving his report, Smokey turned around and went back out to the front yard to post up. Trucho called out to Chino, who was in the back of the house, and put him up on game as far as what was going down. Chino came out of the back room with a Russian AK-47 in his hands.

Everyone was tense as the nine cars that drove down the street came to a stop in front of the house. The tension only grew stronger as no one made any attempt to get out of any of the cars. Chino let out a very loud, unmistakable whistle. At the sound of the whistle, over twenty guns were cocked and raised, aimed at the line of cars. Everyone waited on Chino, who had the AK-47 aimed at the second car. One false move and he was going to send a line of 223s that reached from the first vehicle to the third.

"If shit don't look right, we gonna wake this bitch up!" Chino called out to the soldiers that were close enough to hear him. "And if they don't get out them whips soon, we gonna spray every last fucking car!"

It was as if the occupants of the vehicles also heard the order because a few moments later, every last door of the eight vehicles opened up. Twenty-six angry Mexicans stepped out of their vehicles, all with guns in their hands, ready for their leader to give an order. Their leader stood 5'10" tall and looked like he weighed close to 250 pounds. His long hair was tapered and pulled back into one long braid down his back.

Chino had never seen the young general before, but there was no mistaking who he was. Fat Boy had an air about himself unlike any other Norteños general. He was young but not reckless. Looking at him, most people had a hard time accepting the legend behind his name. He didn't have the menacing look of a lot of seasoned gang bangers. In fact, if he were to remove his tattoos, he could very well pass for not being a gang member period. However, all one needed to do was take a second glance into the eyes behind the prescription glasses in order to see the calculated fierce killer that moved like he was one of the actual founding members of The Norteños Organization. His body count was rumored to be so high, some said he should have been an assassin instead of a field commander.

Chino lowered the assault rifle that was in his hands. He still kept it ready. He didn't care that Fat Boy was a big homie. Chino wasn't bowing down to no mothafucka! If Fat Boy wanted it, he could get it too! Chino stood his ground and waited as Fat Boy made his way over to the house. He walked with the confidence of a proven leader. A man of power.

As Fat Boy made it to the porch, the thought that came to Chino's mind was, he moved more like the mothafuckas half his size. Chino made sure to remember that.

"I came to holla at Blinky." His voice was soft yet commanding.

"Looks more like you came for an invasion instead of a conversation, homie. But you wasted your trip anyway 'cause Blinky can't do no more talking, homie." Chino wasn't about to acknowledge that he knew who Fat Boy was. He decided he would fuck with Fat Boy's head a little bit. "Who are you anyway, homie?"

"I'm the last mothafucka that you or yo' homies wanna be owing money too! That same mothafucka that you mothafuckas were supposed to be dropping a package off to that got intercepted. Right now, though, you can call me Fat Boy." He had a smile on his face as he spoke. But Chino could easily see the danger that was behind his eyes.

"Why don't you come in, homie, so we can talk about this shit. 'Cause standing out here like this ain't 'bout to do shit but potentially get a bunch of mothafuckas hurt."

"And who the fuck are you, homie?"

Chino smiled at the question. "They call me Chino, homie. Right now, you can say I'm the mothafucka in charge. Naturally, that means I'm the mothafucka you want to talk to."

Without pause, Fat Boy walked up the steps. He was followed by his first and second in command. A general and his two colonels. The second one made a call and like magic, all the guns the soldiers that came with them were holding, disappeared.

Chino turned around and led Fat Boy and his two men into the house. They were followed by Casper, Trucho, and Smokey. All of whom had looks on their faces that said they were ready for whatever. Chino led the way to the table inside of the dining room. He was followed by Fat Boy, who took a seat across from Chino. His right-hand man, Scarface, stood off to the left behind Fat Boy. Trucho was positioned behind Chino. Casper, Smokey, and Flacco, Fat Boy's third in command, all took up positions inside of the living room. The tension inside of the house was thick enough to choke on.

Fat Boy was the first to speak. "Brah, I know you said you were in charge right now, but I'm really trynna deal with that fool Blinky. That fool was bumping his mothafuck'n gums on the phone on some tough nigga shit. I came down the freeway to hear some more of that tough ass talk now that a mothafucka done fumbled my fucking package. I wanna see how far he gonna take that tough shit now."

"The problem with tough niggaz is they make so many enemies along the way that when they finally get fucked over, no one knows exactly who fucked them over. I can tell you this, though, that mothafucka ain't gonna be talking that tough shit no more." The air of confidence Chino spoke with and the apparent authority he had over his homies that he was trying to wear on his chest, like a badge of honor, told Fat Boy something about Chino.

"No disrespect to you or nothing, little homie, but that's a big statement for someone even temporarily in charge to make about a commanding officer." He already possessed an idea of what Chino was hinting at, yet Fat Boy was toying with the young warrior to see what his mental diplomacy was like.

"No disrespect to you either, homie, but I've never known a dead man to talk, let alone talk tough." Chino waited for his words to take effect.

Fat Boy sat and thought about the ramifications of Chino's statement. If it did have an effect on the leader, he didn't display any signs of it. The house they were currently in belonged to Blinky. If he were to believe Chino's insinuation that Blinky was dead, the natural assumption would be Chino was the next solider in line and was promoted to take Blinky's spot in the chain of command.

"So, you telling me that Crazy put you in Blinky's spot as the representative of 21st?" Although posed as a question, Chino knew it was more of a challenge from Fat Boy.

"Something like that."

"What do you mean something like that, homie? It's either you've been appointed the authority or haven't!"

Straight Beast Mode 2

"Nobody's heard from the big homie in weeks before Blinky was killed. I was appointed third in command by the big homie. Since ain't nobody heard anything from him, I assumed control until we hear something from the homie. I wasn't about to sit back and let everything go to shit just 'cause the big homie was missing. If I had done that, what would it say about me?"

Fat Boy didn't respond initially. It wasn't normal for a big homie to lose touch with his head soldier. Everyone had heard of Monster's death. If Chino was speaking the truth and Blinky was killed also, that would make two of 21st's top soldiers being killed back-to-back. Plus, their big homie was missing. Something wasn't right. If it was his area, Fat Boy would get to the bottom of this shit ASAP. But it wasn't his area; therefore, it wasn't his business.

"Then I guess I should be turning to you for answers about my shit. Ain't nothing personal, homie, but this set owes me, and I intend to collect my shit."

"I heard about that shit that popped off." Chino tilted his head toward Scarface, who refused to make eye contact with him. "I would've come to you, homie, but I've had my mothafuck'n hands full making sure mothafuckas fell in line and shit didn't get out of hand. The word on the streets is them niggaz from Sunnydale are the ones that jacked yo' boy. If you trynna see them fools about something, I can fully assist you with that. As far as that work you lost, homie, I got something in the works. Give me a couple of weeks and I'll personally take care of that shit for you."

Fat Boy liked how the little homie stepped up to the plate. He didn't make excuses, nor did he try to circumvent the responsibility off to his big homie. He was starting to like Chino.

"I'll tell you what, homie, since you're so G about it, take a month to take care of that. Ain't no rush. Gone ahead and make sure everything is on point with yo' hood. And when you hit me, just make it half of what it was supposed to be. Consider it my acknowledgment to your leadership initiative. As far as that other shit goes, I appreciate the offer, but we don't need no support or assistance, lil' homie. Just give me the info and the address if you got it, and I'll do the rest. You can consider this a heads-up. MMN 'bout to act up in your area." The smiling fat nigga that looked jolly and innocent somehow managed to disappear. Chino was staring in the eyes of a seasoned general, a full-blooded, stone-cold killer.

The look didn't faze Chino. As far as he was concerned, the world was full of killers, especially in the hood. Chino's philosophy was simple, *"Everybody could be a killer, and killers were killers until they got killed."*

Fat Boy beckoned Scarface over to him with the flick of his wrist. He whispered something in Scarface's ear. Immediately, Scarface left and went to carry out the order.

"I just told him to have the rest of them fools disperse and take the heat off of your spot. My three lieutenants will stay so we can discuss everything you know about the mothafuckas that thought they played me. Then I'mma teach them mothafuckas a lesson that this whole city gonna learn." The look in Fat Boy's eyes made it crystal clear he meant what he said.

Chino looked over and made eye contact with Trucho, who had been paying close attention to Chino the entire time. The signal was so subtle that no one in the room caught it except Fat Boy. Trucho walked out the front door and made a loud whistle. It told everyone from 21st everything was cool. They were to continue on with whatever they were doing before Fat Boy and his entourage pulled up. Now that the bullshit was out of the way, it was time to get down to business.

Things were going just the way Chino had planned. Fat Boy had no idea. He thought it was really the E-Mobb niggaz who jacked Scarface. He was so eager to get revenge that he ate Chino's story up with no problems. Chino wanted Fat Boy and the MMN homies to declare war on TIO. With Lil' Dooka focused on fighting wars on two different fronts, it would leave room for Chino to take over Sunnydale drug market. Chino had big plans for 21st. He was doing a lot of foul shit, but in his mind, it was all for the good of La Familia.

Chapter 3

When the report of multiple shootings came over the radio, Sgt. M. Dudley, the lead detective over the Gang Taskforce, already knew it was one of his. There was so much beef on the streets of his district between all the rival gangs that it would take an act of God for a homicide to occur and it not be gang related. Dudley and his lead, Detective Morgan, were already headed over to Sunnydale for some follow-up work on a case they were working on, when the call came through.

Sgt. Dudley figured it would be best to get an early start on the new case rather than putting the old case first. After all, it wasn't like the old case was going anywhere anytime soon. He'd learned to be patient and allow nature to take its course, and one way that happened were the snitches. Sgt. Dudley learned early on in his career that he could always expect the snitches to come out of the woodworks for serious crimes. He himself found it amusing that these guys ran the streets playing Cocaine Cowboys and as soon as the law got involved, they were quick to sing as if they were auditioning for a spot on the TV show *American Idol*. It was hilarious.

Sgt. Dudley pulled the Dodge Charger over and parked. The street and sidewalk were filled with onlookers, as always. People who had nothing better to do with their time than to eagerly search for information that would supply their daily gossip.

"Two-to-one odds that at least 70 percent of these people know exactly what happened and why it happened. Yet no one is going to tell us shit. They'll gossip and talk about it like it was the latest episode of one of them trashy soap operas. All while they will cry the same song about the police not doing anything to clean the neighborhood up. Never once would it occur to any one of them that there's nothing we can do when they refuse to cooperate. Hell, even once we get a suspect in custody the witnesses develop amnesia."

Morgan had heard this same song hundreds of times already. It was Sgt. Dudley's number one complaint. Without fail, he would vent the same discomfort at every last crime scene.

"Mathew, honestly, could you blame them? If you lived in one of these neighborhoods, could you honestly say you would risk the lives of your loved ones by giving a statement to the police? And risk someone coming along and making a name for themselves by killing you and your entire family."

"If these people would work with us in cleaning up the streets, there wouldn't be any more of these low-life mother-fuckers around to do anything about it." He said this just as they were walking by Waka, Fayzo, and Samantha.

When the three TIO members heard what Sgt. Dudley said, Waka nudged him hard while saying, "Bitch-ass mothafuckas!" loud enough for him to hear.

Sgt. Dudley didn't pay the comment any attention. He kept right along talking while Det. Morgan asked him, "At what cost to innocent civilian lives does it take achieve our version of a ghetto Utopia? The truth of the matter is right now the majority of the killings that transpire are all the gang members and drug dealers themselves. With an innocent causality every so often in the mix. I'm sure those same people whom you speak of notice this as well. And, in fact, I'm quite sure it has something to do with their reluctance to step up. After all, there's no need to endanger their own family when the street low lives will continue to kill each other anyway.

"Fuck, Morgan! I swear, sometimes it seems like you are more interested in defending these people than you are wanting justice."

And sometimes I silently think you are just as bad as the low lives themselves. Of course, she didn't say this thought out loud. Instead, her response was, "It's not my job to uphold justice, Mathew. That's for the courts. My job is to uphold the law and apprehend suspects."

Detective Morgan was a middle-aged woman that still looked like she was in her 20s. At 5'4" and weighing 130 pounds, she gave people the impression of being harmless. Especially with a smile that would light up any room she walked into. However, the sweet, pretty innocence masked a fierce and tough personality. One that had helped her gain the respect of both her peers as well as the gang bangers on the street, who couldn't help always discussing the new

Straight Beast Mode 2

cutie pie detective that didn't take any shit. She transferred over from one of the local sheriff departments two years ago and had quickly cut out her own niche in the world of gang activity investigations.

Sgt. Dudley ignored the last comment from his star detective. He wasn't about to get into another one of their many long debates over the ethics of law enforcement. Morgan often reminded him of one of the early 90's, in the closet, liberal lesbian bitches that were always crying about equal rights and warmer nights and a bunch of other bullshit just like the fucking niggers themselves. The truth being, he didn't like being challenged on anything, let alone his views. Especially by a woman. However, he lacked the self-assurance and know-how to deal with it. Therefore, as he often did when he couldn't face the realities of his own inequities, he blamed the other party. Often making up something ugly and hateful about the person just to make his dislike of them easily acceptable to himself.

They made their way past the yellow crime scene caution tape. Crime Scene Investigations was on the scene. Sgt. Dudley didn't bother wasting his time with pleasantries with the other investigators or even formalities. He walked through the crime scene like he was there alone. Lost in his own world.

The first thing Sgt. Dudley noticed were the spent gun casings outside of apartment 187. He took a brief detour from the front of the apartment. Making his way over to the corner of the building, where more markers indicated more bullet shell casings. The casings were only at the bottom of the stairs. This told the sergeant that whatever took place at the apartment was interrupted by new shooters, who no doubt came to the aid of the victims inside of the apartment.

Unfortunately, the victims were already taken away to the hospital by the paramedics. Sgt. Dudley would have loved to have a few minutes with them. Experience had taught him that sometimes if the right amount of pressure was applied, he could get some victims to slip and divulge a sliver of information they might not have necessarily divulged had they been in a normal state of mind.

From the shell casing markers, he noticed at least three to five different shooters. He continued to look over the scene, making mental notes and writing things down on paper. He made his way over to where the fist body was found. More shell casings were scattered on the floor. Some lay atop pools of blood. Sgt. Dudley took it all in. Det. Morgan had just finished having a discussion with the responding officers. Sgt. Dudley sensed her presence as she approached.

"Where are the guns, Morgan? I count at least four different shooters, but I've yet to see one fucking gun. Did those incompetent fucks from crime scene fuck with my scene and remove the fucking guns?" Dudley never took his eyes or his attention away from the scene, taking it in.

"I just finished speaking with the responding officers. They're reporting that they didn't find any guns at all on the scene when they arrived." This got Dudley's attention.

He looked up from what he was doing. "You're telling me, Morgan, that those idiots let someone walk off with the most important pieces of evidence from this crime scene?"

"By their calculations, it took the first officers on the scene four minutes and twenty-three seconds to arrive. They stated there was the normal number of spectators already on scene when they arrived. However, no one seemed overly suspicious. Neither was there anyone lingering too close to the actual crime scene when the officers arrived."

Dudley chewed this information over in his head. Somebody had removed the guns from the crime scene before the officers arrived. In Dudley's mind, it would only stand to reason that it was the victims' friends that removed the guns. The original shooters wouldn't have reason to remove them. Plus, as it appears, they were chased away from the apartment. Which meant they didn't have time to stop and retrieve the victims' guns, or anything else from the apartment.

He stood up. "Come on, Morgan, I've seen enough."

In fact, Sgt. Dudley had seen more than enough. There was no question as to what had transpired. He knew the two victims well.

MoMo and TG were both active members of Tear It Off. Dudley was aware that this was not only the late Auntie Dee's apartment, but it was also one of the main hangouts of the gang. Dudley also knew it was a safe assumption that members of the small yet elite 357 Mobb were the ones responsible for today's shooting. In all probability, the 357 Mobb were the perpetrators responsible for Auntie Dee's death as well.

Detective Morgan followed Sgt. Dudley as he made his way back to their car. She couldn't help the slight pull of emotions that threatened to tug at her heart as she thought of all of the young men and women whose lives were stolen from them all too early due to the rise in street and gang violence. So many young and lost souls, taken too early. Robbed of the chance to experience so many different things that life had to offer. As she climbed into the Charger, she silently said a prayer thanking God that she was alive and still healthy.

***

Thick, cool fog covered the Bay Area and lingered in the streets. Bay Area residents had their own name for the thick clouds that blanketed its city streets. They called it Bay Fog. At times it was known to be so thick in the early morning that a person couldn't see a foot in front of their face. It was this same fog that covered the grounds of the cemetery this early morning.

Rick stared at the name placard covering the grave, grief struck with emotions. He'd been at the grave site since sunrise. It was now going on 7:30 a.m. For Rick, the laws of time didn't exist. Mentally and emotionally, he had been stuck inside of a horrific time capsule for years. Lost in memories. Haunted by the shadows of "what if" along with thoughts of "if only."

She was his queen, his world, his everything. The woman that he was supposed to build and spend the rest of his life with. Unfortunately, life never goes the way that we want or expect it to go. Something or somebody always seemed to get in the way and fuck things up.

Fresh tears began sliding down his face again. Even after all of these years, the pain was just as sharp as it was on that day. That day he had first received the tragic news.

He reached up and wiped his face with the palm of his hand. He took a couple of long deep breaths to help himself slowly start to regain his composure. Once again, that familiar ice-cold feeling that has filled his body for the last fifteen years began to slowly wash over his body. Once again, his veins began to fill with artic-cold ice water. Replacing the blood.

"Don't worry, baby. I'm taking care of shit. On everything I love, them mothafuckas gonna know what pain feels like when I'm done!" The sworn declaration was more to himself than it was to the lifeless grave he stood over.

Rick clenched both of his fists into tight balls as he gathered himself and his composure. His temper was one of Rick's biggest downfalls. It had cost him so much throughout his life already. Which was the only reason he now tried to keep some sort of containment on the rage that laid just below the surface of his resolve.

He made his way back to his vehicle, noticing that the sun had fully risen in the sky. The warmth of the sun's rays cooled against the surface of his skin. Skin that was chilled from the icy blood flowing through his veins. Rick never looked at his niece as he climbed inside of the back seat. As she started the car and drove off, Rick pulled out his cell phone and placed a call. He knew the person on the other end of the line would deeply enjoy what he was about to tell her.

"It's quite unusual for you to be calling me this early in the morning. Are you finally calling to tell a girl that you are going to make my dreams come true and let me see just how good all of that fine chocolate is going to taste in my mouth?" Her voice dripped of pure, sweet honey. He couldn't detect not a hint of the venomous poison he knew she was full of.

"Girl, don't you start none of that nonsense of yours early this morning. I'mma make one of yo' dreams come true alright, but it ain't gonna be none of that shit that you got on your mind. So, let it go." Rick wasn't in the mood for any bullshit.

Straight Beast Mode 2

    Normally her flirtatious advances wouldn't bother him. Every chance she got she was flirting with him. She'd been doing it for so long that he normally would ignore it. Not today though. Not when his trip down memory lane caused emotions of anger and rage to overtake both his mind and body. The only thing he could focus on was rage.
    The girl on the other end of the phone, with the Harley Quinn hairdo, could feel his rage coming through the phone. Like some sort of wild beast stalking through the jungle in search of some sort of outlet of relief. She sat up in her bed and got serious.
    "Okay, Daddy, I'm all ears. What's up?" The tone of her voice reflected her newfound serious mind state.
    "It's time we speed shit up some. I want you to dig deep inside your bag of tricks and make your presence known."
    She smiled and licked her lips as her pussy became wet. The prospect of violence was what she lived for. To her it was the best aphrodisiac in the world. Her left hand dropped involuntarily to her lap. She began running her fingers up and down, over the material of her now soaking wet thong.
    "Mmm, Daddy, I've been waiting for you to make this call. I'mma get right on it." She paused for a brief second. Her middle finger now pressing firmly against her clit. She added, "I promise you, Daddy, you are going to love what I do for you too."
    "I better." Rick knew her like the back of his hand. He knew what she was doing while they were talking. He could hear the way the lust made her voice a little huskier.
    He knew that violence and talk of violence turned the young psychopath on. In his mind, he could see her strumming her fingers across her little wet pussy. More importantly, though, he knew she would make good on her promise. She would make him proud.
    "You keep doing what I need you to do and soon, you just may find me doing what you need me to do." At the sound of that, a vision of him finally sliding his big black dick into her popped into her head. Causing an orgasm to instantly explode in her body.
    Rick heard her trying to contain the loud moan that wanted to escape her lips because of the violent orgasm. He hung up just

before the moans succeeded in escaping. He closed his eyes and smiled.

The name of the young, white, psychopathic, deranged woman who looked and acted like Harley Quinn was named Zoey Poppins. He knew one hundred percent without a doubt she would get it popping!

Chapter 4

Budda had everything he planned on taking home with him packed already. He received word almost two and half hours ago that his bail had been posted. He was just waiting for the jail to finalize the paperwork in order for him to be released. The wait would have gotten under the skin of most inmates. When a mothafucka was locked up, the only three things constantly on his mind were food, pussy, and freedom. Once that release date came around, every minute of the day felt like years ticking away on the clock. Budda wasn't an inmate, though. He was a street nigga that adopted the discipline and behavior of old convicts. One of the disciplines he'd acquired was patience. The two-and-a-half-hour wait didn't bother him like most. All that mattered to Budda was the fact that he was being released.

For the past few months, he sat in his cell feeling hopeless as he received report after report from the streets of his niggaz getting smashed. He knew they needed him. It was his only reason for bailing out. During the beginning of the war with the 357 Mobb, he was leaning on the fence as to whether he would bail out or leave everything to Lil' Dooka. Auntie Dee getting killed made the decision for him. Her death hit him harder than a punch from Iron Mike Tyson. When he heard the news, he instantly gave the word for his people to begin taking the steps to bail him out.

As if things weren't already fucked up enough. An hour ago, while at recreation, he just heard the news about MoMo and TG. The news had Budda ready to get on anything moving!

Finally, the deputy came over the wall intercom in his cell and told him to roll his shit up. That was jailhouse lingo that meant pack your shit. He had finally made bail. Budda didn't waste any time. The only thing he took with him was his pictures and mail from his loved ones.

None of his niggaz got mad at him as they watched him walk across the dayroom and out of the unit without saying a word to any of them. They all already knew what time it was and what page Budda was on. This surely was about to be the coldest winter ever!

***

Murda walked into the living room with two bottles of chilled Hennessy in his hands that he had just grabbed out of the freezer. He made his way over to the couch and sat down next to C1ty. Murda sat one of the bottles down on the coffee table in front of his cousin. He cracked the top on the second bottle and took a long swallow. The ice-cold liquid was comfortingly delicious as it slid down his dry throat.

Neither of the men had said a word since they left the gunfight at the bitch Auntie Dee's apartment. They'd driven all the way out to Filmore. Murda had a little bitch that stayed over on Filmore named Kia. They'd come to her spot because shit was too hot for them to try and stay in Double Rock.

Kia was a true city bitch. Murda knew she knew enough not to try and be all up in their shit. The bitch would mind her business and play her position. Murda called her as they were driving over to let her know he was coming thru. When they got to her place, Kia didn't mention the fact that Murda never told her that he had someone with him. She was solid like that.

After letting them in, she walked to the back room and came back out with an ounce of Purple Kush and some Honey Bourbon Backwoods. She gave both to Murda before going into the kitchen to make something to eat. She would leave them be until either Murda called her or whenever whatever she was cooking was ready. This was good because right now, the last thing Murda needed was a bitch fucking with him.

On the outside Murda and C1ty both just seemed to be in quiet moods. However, under the surface they both were fuming. No, boiling! They had driven over to the Sunnydale Projects with nothing but murder on their minds and in their hearts. Both men felt that they were robbed when them bitch-ass niggaz came to the aid of the two niggaz they had caught slipping inside of Dee's apartment.

C1ty lit the blunt he had finished rolling and took a long couple of deep pulls on it. His eyes were closed. Inside of C1ty's mind he

Straight Beast Mode 2

was replaying the image of the blast from the Mossberg knocking MoMo smoothly off his feet. *Well*, he thought to himself, *it wasn't smoothly off his feet!* It was more like MoMo had been snatched or torn off of his feet. C1ty hit the blunt again, savoring the look of utter shock and pure fear that was on MoMo's face once he realized what was going on. The fear was so thick as it rushed from his body that C1ty could actually taste it.

The sweet taste of MoMo's fear slowly gave way to the vile taste of defeat. As the images of he and Murda being interrupted from the kill intruded his vision next.

"Fuck!" His frustration verbally showed itself. C1ty leaned all the way back on the couch. His eyes remained closed. Head tilted back like Stevie Wonder.

"Shit, nigga, speak on it." Murda already knew what was wrong. He was just giving his cousin an avenue in case he wanted to get the shit off his chest.

"My nigga, you already know. Shit was right in a niggaz fingertips. Then, all of a sudden, pulled right the fuck out of a niggaz reach." Even though Kia was a solid bitch, C1ty still spoke in code. If his ship ever sank, it wasn't going to be behind loose lips.

Murda was lighting his blunt as C1ty spoke. He tilted his head back and blew the smoke up to the ceiling. "You know I don't too much fuck with that God nigga. But blood, it seems like some niggaz be so mothafuck'n lucky, that the only explanation is, God had their mothafuck'n back."

"I don't have no problems with God, my nigga. I just know that he needs to stay the fuck out of my business." C1ty reached inside of his pocket for his phone, which started ringing.

His older brother Dell's name was on the display when C1ty looked at the screen. "Speak on it, big brah," he answered the call.

"What's up, lil' brah? Them white folks finally released Wes's personal shit today. I went down and picked it up a little earlier."

G-Baby had been trying to get Wes's personal effects for over a week. They wouldn't let her get his shit because she wasn't immediate family.

"That's good, brah. I was getting tired of hearing about all of the shit them mothafuckas was sending my baby through." C1ty was glad Dell decided to handle it because he himself wasn't in the right state of mind to be dealing with people.

"I went through his phone to try and see if I could get an idea of what he was up to that night. He got a call from somebody right around the time shit supposedly jumped off. When I hit the number from my phone some lil' bitch answered. I'mma run the bitch license plates and see what's good. I'll holla when I find something." Dell sounded like he hoped he found something out of pocket about whoever the little bitch was.

C1ty couldn't blame his older brother. Shit, right now all of them were looking for the slightest reasons to take their pain out on somebody. Which was why C1ty was so mad that he was robbed of his kill earlier.

"Alright, bet, let me know what it do. Have you talked to Don today?" C1ty hadn't spoken with Don since the funeral.

"Naaw, brah, that nigga ain't answering his phone. I left the nigga a message yesterday, but he ain't hit a nigga back. I'mma swing by his spot later and make sure he alright though."

"Fa'sho. If I don't hear back from you tonight, I'mma tap in wit' you tomorrow. I need to hook up and go over shit anyway."

"Off top, brah, tap in, it's good. We'll link up." On the other end of the phone, Dell could hear in C1ty's voice that his little brother was hurting harder than he was showing. He knew mothafuckas needed to pay for what happened to Wes, and he was going to make sure they did.

Kia came walking into the living room carrying a plate of food in her hands as C1ty was getting off the phone with Dell.

"Is he eating, baby?" she asked Murda as she sat his plate down on the coffee table in front of him.

Murda replied without asking C1ty if was hungry or not. "Yeah, he's eating. This family, so if I'm eating, then he eating."

"I know that's right, Daddy," Kia replied. She stood up from setting the plate down and walked back into the kitchen to go fix a plate for C1ty.

Straight Beast Mode 2

C1ty wasn't trying to be disrespectful, but Kia had an ass so big she sort of leaned forward when she walked. The way her big ole booty was swallowing her yoga pants, C1ty could tell she wasn't wearing any panties. He bet it would feel good to get behind that big ole booty.

"Cousin, we both know G-Baby would kill you ten times for ever thinking about it," Murda teased him. He couldn't fault his cousin for staring. Kia's ass was bigger than all of them Kardashian bitches, and shit was real.

"Nigga, the way that big ole juicy mothafucka look, if G-Baby was here she'd be watching that mothafucka with me. Why you playing, nigga!" C1ty didn't know whether shit was true or not, but in his mind, he could actually see the shit happening.

Murda bust out laughing. Kia was in her early thirties. She had what niggaz often referred to as "honey brown" skin. She had a pretty average looking face with a sweet smile. She stood about 5'6" and had a body that looked like it came out of the backwoods of North Carolina somewhere. California had some bad bitches, but none of them were built like Kia.

The only other time C1ty could ever recall seeing a booty like the one Kia had was when he was locked up looking at a *Viral Magazine*. He'd seen a bitch that was so thick he jacked-off to her every night for a week straight. The bitch name was Ms. Panda or some shit like that. Kia came walking back into the room with a plate of food in her hands for C1ty.

"Murda, let me find out you in here talking shit about my cooking," she said halfheartedly as she walked in.

C1ty didn't pay too much attention to her the first time she came in. So, he had missed what he was seeing now. Her pussy was phat, and it looked like she had a sock in her pants. The material of the light gray yoga pants outlined her pussy like they had been painted on her. C1ty could feel his dick getting hard.

"Now you know ain't shit a nigga could ever say about your food. A nigga in here laughing 'cause the way my little cousin was looking at all that ass you got. A nigga didn't know if he wanted a

38

plate of food to eat or you." Murda laughed even harder at his own joke.

"Is that right?" She looked from Murda to C1ty and stood back to her legs, popping her ass out. "Well listen, sugar, I suggest you take this plate of food here because your young ass couldn't begin to handle this here good loving. Ask him, he will tell you. It's so good his ass be all goo-goo-ga-ga'ing, like a little baby when I whip it on his ass."

Murda couldn't do shit but laugh even harder because that shit was as true as the Holy Gospel.

When Kia sat C1ty's plate down, she purposely bent over so that her ass was right in his face. C1ty could see the silhouette of her pussy lips as clear as day.

She looked back at him from over her shoulder with a smile on her face. "Trust and believe, sugar, that forbidden fruit that Adam ate in the Garden of Eden wasn't no damn apple."

This time when Murda laughed he doubled over. Kia started giggling before smacking herself on the ass. Then her giggles turned into laughter as well.

"Don't get me wrong, ma. Yo' shit look good enough to be wrapped in a package of some shit called 'temptation,' but the only forbidden fruit I'm ever gonna eat is in the Garden of G-Baby. If it ain't the wife, it ain't right." C1ty leaned forward and picked up the plate of food. Ignoring the big ole booty in front of him. Fuck what Murda was talking about. Something that big you didn't call an ass. It was a Booty with a capital 'B.'

"I know that's right! Talk that shit then, sugar," Kia responded as she stood up. She respected that he was gangsta for that shit.

She didn't miss the size of the print in his pants before she turned around. Judging from the size of the print, a blind bitch could see that the little nigga liked what he saw. She did too. Like it or not, she wasn't that kind of bitch. She and Murda liked to joke around, but she was a real southern girl. Loyal to the tee. Kia gave Murda a kiss before walking out.

"Little mothafucka must think he's Dolemite or somebody," she mumbled to herself as she left.

Straight Beast Mode 2

When Kia was gone and C1ty was done laughing at her comment about him being Dolemite, he took a bite of the delicious southern fried chicken and said, "Shorty wild as hell, my nigga."

"Fresh out da jungle, nigga, you know how I like 'em," Murda replied.

De'Kari

Chapter 5

"Yeah, yeah, whatever nigga! Save the jokes, nigga, I don't know what it is about that lucky ass nigga. Brother, you already know how I be tearing shit up. But every time I bet that chimney ass nigga.... blood, I can't beat that nigga fo' shit...." Kino laughed as he listened to his brother FL rant and rave about losing another bet to a nigga he met up in the county named J.

FL met J about two years ago, and the two of them hit it off instantly. Their mutual love for gambling gave the two of them something in common. That and their competitive nature. The two of them bet on everything from professional sporting events and games to boxing matches and mixed martial arts fights. Shit, if niggaz started fighting in the jail they would bet on who would win. For the most part, their betting and payouts were pretty much even. J won his fair share and FL won his. When it came to the NFL games and poker, FL just couldn't seem to get any luck. J kicked his ass like O-Dog did that nigga in *Menace II Society*.

"Brother, all I'm saying is if a nigga is always kicking my ass at something, I'm either gonna get some kind of edge to even shit out, or I'll fuck with him on everything else except for what the nigga keeps kicking my ass in." Kino knew he was he was getting under FL's skin, but he didn't give a fuck. The shit was funny as hell to him.

Losing the money wasn't the issue. Their whole squad was "upgame." Money wasn't a problem, FL just hated losing. He couldn't accept that shit!

"Yeah, yeah, whatever nigga! First off, nigga, ain't nobody kicking yo' ass. That ain't gonna happen. That nigga just got bit by the luck bug or some shit like that. Just send that nigga his five bands to Cash App and save that comedy shit for niggaz that's actually funny, nigga. 'Cause you ain't."

"You have one minute left on your call." The voice recording interrupted their conversation.

"It's all good, brother. You know the kid got you. I'mma fly that ASAP. Soon as we done. But on some real shit, when I come out to rec tonight you better know when to hold'em and know when to fold'em. Or I'mma have some more jokes for yo' ass." Kino popped two Facebook triple-stack ecstasy pills in his mouth and chased them down his throat with some Mali water.

"Yeah, yeah, whatever nigga. Tell sis I said I love her, nigga." FL had a smile on his face. "I love you, nigga."

"I love you too, brother," Kino replied just before the line went dead.

He put the phone in the pocket of his Prada jacket. He took another swallow of the Mali water. Kino was feeling himself, as Mac Dre would say. He was thirty-two years old but still had that "I'm invincible" feeling that all niggaz had at twenty-one.

He was 6'1", 210 pounds on an athletic frame. With his light skin, long, skinny dread locks and pretty boy features, he looked more like an urban clothing model than the vicious killer that he was. His features came from his mother's genes. His father was African American, but his mother was full-blooded Nicaraguan.

Kino and FL were like night and day. FL had long thick dreadlocks and root beer brown skin. He could pass as a double for the rapper Mozzy from Sacramento. FL was the quiet type. Twice as deadly as a Black Mamba or venomous water moccasin. Kino, on the other hand, was the flamboyant live wire type. Just as deadly but twice as dangerous, because a nigga wouldn't suspect him to be the Candy Man type. Those same niggaz never lived to regret underestimating him.

Kino was seated in the driver seat of his Mercedes AMG 550. He was parked in A-lot of the Sunnydale Housing Projects. A-lot was known as the Four-Deuce home of the Down Below Mafia, and Kino was one of the leaders of the Mafia. Originally it was just known as Down Below. The handle "Mafia" would later be added to the moniker because of the Mafia or Mobb type way they went about killing their enemies over the years. A younger Kino played a big part in those killings in the early days. His mother tried her best to raise a young Kino right. But when you were raised Down Below there was a better chance of the Devil getting into Heaven than there was of you getting out of Hell.

Straight Beast Mode 2

Another name used when referring to the Down Below was simply Low. Just like Tre-4, Down Below inside of the Sunnydale Projects. This project community was built on a hill. 4-2 was the side of the projects that was located at the bottom of the hill. 3-4 was located at the top of the hill. When the Sunnydale Projects were united, it reigned supreme in the Underworld of San Francisco. One thing led to another, and a Civil War broke out inside of the projects. A war that would last over a decade and divide the projects.

This ongoing war between neighbors, friends, and family was not only one of the weirdest in San Francisco's history. It had also been one of the most dangerous. On any given Sunday a niggaz own neighbor could just open fire as a mothafucka came home at night. The funk was essentially 24-7 when the OP lived in the same complex as you did. Sunnydale Projects was Hell indeed.

This would explain why a baby Draco sat nicely on Kino's lap while he sat in his Benz. In Hell a demon could pop up at any given time. Some demons were friends, some were foes. So, a nigga stayed on his toes.

"Bitch, get low!" He gave the command to the little Dominican chick that was in his passenger seat.

Even if he hadn't picked up the baby Draco and cocked it back, the sound of Kino's voice was enough to send chills over her succulent body and scare her into action. Rosalinda was born and raised in East Palo Alto. She knew hesitation at the wrong time could easily cost a person their life when they lived in or around the killing fields.

She slid the passenger seat backward as fast as it would go while trying to get down as low as she could in the space beneath the dashboard in front of the passenger seat. The size of her nice, phat Latin ass was making the task difficult. As she wiggled to get her ass as far as it would go under the dash, her eyeglasses fell off her face. She began saying a silent prayer, begging God not to let this be the day she left the earth.

Kino didn't pay attention to any of Rosalinda's actions. His attention was on the caravan of vehicles he saw driving up the street. He was aware of the beef between the TIO niggaz from the 4 and the 357 niggaz from Double Rock. Shit, the Tre-4 niggaz had a list of niggaz they were beefing wit', including the Low. Kino was on point because the Low had their share of niggaz they were beefing with as well. Kino refused to ever be one of the niggaz that the sucka side caught slipping.

As he watched the cars, the hairs on his arms and the back of his neck stood up. In the hood the only time cars rode back-to-back-to-back was during funerals, sideshows, and when shit was about to pop the fuck off. Auntie Dee's funeral was last week, and he hadn't heard shit about no fucking sideshows.

Kino wasn't a dummy. He knew what time it was. Somebody thought it was Drill Season. Well, they picked the right nigga at the right mothafuck'n time. In this situation, most niggaz would've reached for the phone and got some niggaz outside quick as fuck. Kino wasn't that kind of nigga. He wasn't worried about niggaz coming to help. His help was in his mothafuck'n hands! He reached for the handle of the door.

***

The little bitch's head was so good Young Stubby had to bite down on his lip just to keep himself from moaning like some little bitch. Stubby was way too gangsta for that shit. The little Mexican bitch was sucking his dick so good. She could give dick sucking lessons to porn stars. Superhead herself ain't never sucked a dick this good. Stubby was in a trance-like state watching his dick disappear in the bitch's mouth only to reappear seconds later drenched in spit. His balls tingled from slapping back and forth on her chin. He closed his eyes and tilted his head back as he felt the muscles in his abdomen tighten in preparation for the nutt he was about to bust.

He swayed left and right on his feet. His balance was off slightly as his body began to drift down the highway to delirium!

Suddenly, his body jerked as he was snatched from the brink of bliss and transported back to the bowels of hell. The unmistakable sound of gunfire that had erupted outside of his building was responsible for the sudden change.

The little bitch kept right on sucking the life out of his dick. She was lost in her own pleasuristic world. Oblivious of the sounds of rapid gunfire that betrayed what could only be a very intense gun battle. She had two fingers buried deep inside of her pussy while her thumb assaulted her clitoris. She made a whining sound as Stubby pulled away from her, snatching his dick out of her mouth.

A look of confusion was on the bitch's face as her fingers continued their assault on her throbbing pussy. The look on her face was desperate as her eyes pleaded for Stubby to ram his dick back down her throat. That all changed as she watched him pull the biggest gun she had ever in her life seen out of the closet. Lust was immediately replaced with fear, and she wondered what was going on.

Stubby pulled the slide back on the AK-47 and headed straight for the door. As he was storming across the room, the window shattered, sending glass flying everywhere. The Mexican bitch screamed at the top of her lungs. She was still down on her knees. Now, she crouched down as low as she could, cowering with fear. Stubby hadn't even flinched when the windows shattered. He had been in too many gun battles to count. The fiery hot bullets that whistled as they flew thru the air didn't seem to faze him.

Stubby opened the door and stepped outside with the AK raised and ready. A line of vehicles had stopped right in the middle of Sunnydale Ave. It had to be at least five cars that Stubby could see. Mothafuckas were either shooting through the open windows of the vehicles or leaning partially out of opened doors. Stubby couldn't be sure, but the shooters looked to be Mexicans.

Stubby crouched down low like an army soldier and ran over to a Yukon Denali that was parked in A-lot. As he did, he took notice of Kino, who was on the other side of the lot taking cover behind D'Smooth's Cadillac Escalade. Once he was in a secured position, Stubby aimed at the lead vehicle and squeezed the trigger. The mighty roar of the choppa was louder than the rest of the gunshots.

Being a seasoned vet in the art of street war, Stubby knew that if he dismantled the front vehicle or its driver, then the rest of the vehicles would have a shit load of problems trying to get out of the area when they were ready. He also knew that his niggaz were just like he was. They would hear the gun battle that was going on, grab their shit, and come join the battle. Therefore, taking out the mothafuckas in the front was a priority.

After a few seconds of firing, he ducked back down behind the Denali. He heard the sharp piercing ting, ting sound of bullets crashing into and ricocheting off the body of the Denali. Stubby's heart raced, and his breathing was deep and heavy. A wild look came into his eyes, yet he was as calm as a gentle breeze on a warm spring day. Stubby was built for this gangsta shit.

***

(Meanwhile)

Kino didn't see Stubby when he came out of his apartment. He was too busy getting out of the way of the bullets flying over and past his head. When Kino first got out of his car, the shooting had started. The people in the vehicles hadn't noticed him. In fact, they didn't take the time, it seemed to Kino, to notice anything. He opened fire on the entire projects. Kino didn't bother taking aim at anyone or anything in particular. He pointed the baby Draco at the line of vehicles and opened fire. He waved the Draco back and forth along the line of vehicles.

The shooters in the street were caught off guard at first. Kino even heard some of them cry out as his bullets tore into them. When some of them realized the general area the return fire was coming from, they sent a barrage of bullets in search of him. The sound of the AK-47 was music to his ears since the distraction it came from sounded like some much-needed assistance. Kino was relieved. He looked to his left, the direction the sound of the AK-47 came from. He saw Stubby standing by the back end of the Yukon letting the choppa dance.

Immediately, Kino stepped out from behind the Escalade and sent some more hot shit at the mothafuckas who he now saw were Mexicans. Rosalinda's loud screams coming out of the open Mercedes door were not the only screams that could be heard in between

Straight Beast Mode 2

bursts of gunfire. Windows were being shot out left and right. Inside of Stubby's apartment, the other Latina chick stayed crouched down in the same exact spot she was in when Stubby ran out of the front door. Tears came down her cheeks and dripped off of her chin. They splashed in the pool of urine that had collected underneath her. It sounded to her young ears like the United States Army declared war on the housing projects.

A loud, sharp whistle pierced through the air. It was so loud it was heard over the gunfire. Instantly, Mexicans that were standing out of some of the vehicles began piling back inside. The ones who were brave enough to still shoot out of the windows that were rolled down did. Others that weren't so brave were cowering down inside of vehicles. Their guns long since had run out of bullets.

Tires burned rubber on the street as the lead vehicle peeled off. The other vehicles sped off right behind it! Broken glass and hot bullet shells littered the streets where the line of vehicles were just parked. Here and there along the streets were drops of blood left by shooters who weren't fortunate enough to dodge all of the bullets.

As Fat Boy leaned back in the passenger seat, he pulled the red bandana that he had covering the lower half of his face completely off. He didn't know if anyone had been shot or not! He assumed someone did get shot, considering the number of bullets they shot. If someone did or didn't, it didn't bother him in the least. A look of satisfaction was on his face anyway. Once word of what just happened spread, mothafuckas would know in San Francisco and everywhere else in the Bay Area not to fuck with MMN. That's all that mattered.

De'Kari

Chapter 6

By now, Sgt. Dudley had seen so many different forms of violence and outright cruelty within the streets of his Bayview Hunters Point District that nothing really surprised the gang task force sergeant any longer. When he and Detective Morgan pulled up to the scene of the shootout that had taken place on Sunnydale Avenue, it was just another day at the office for him.

When the shootout came over the airways, it wasn't surprising to him that the once feared housing projects had now fallen prey to the same animalistic violence that its residences had once wreaked upon the streets. The report of twenty-plus shooting victims didn't even give the sergeant pause. In his mind, if you lived by sword you died by the sword. And as for the so-called innocent victims, if you laid down with dogs, you were bound to catch fleas.

In Sergeant Dudley's mind all niggers were animals of some sort or the other. Fuck'em and good riddance was what he thought.

The sight of so many numbered placards that were spread out along the street inside the parking lot of the housing project sent chills up and down Detective Morgan's small body. She knew the mean streets of San Francisco could be cruel. Yet to her, this was a different degree of cruelty. Majority of the victims that were reportedly taken to hospitals for treatment of gunshots were women and young children. Kids who just so happened to be playing outside in the housing projects. Or even inside what should have been the safe confines of their apartments. Tragic victims who by no means had any ties or connections to the street life or whatever the cause was for today's violence.

As always, there were many onlookers. The street was crowded with them. Nosey, low-life, Section 8 housing mothafuckas who had nothing else better to do with themselves or their time. Then to stand around and watch them work. As if they gave a fuck. To Sgt. Dudley there was no way any of them could possibly give a fuck. If they did, someone, anyone, would come forward as a witness. Someone would take a stand and say enough was enough.

He looked around at the people as if he half expected someone to telepathically receive his message and come forth to give a statement of facts. The only thing he received was an odd sense of foolishness. That, if even for a second, he could let himself think that these animals would do the right thing and help not only themselves but the members of their chicken-shit community.

Feeling somewhat like a jackass, Sgt. Dudley started to turn his attention away from the crowd of spectators and back to his job. Until his eyes landed on a very familiar face. He smiled to himself then made his way over to the face.

"You know, I've never been what you may consider a gambling man. But if I had to bet, I would bet that your boyfriend or his crew of so-called brothers had something to do with this." He made his fingers in the form of quotations when he said the words "so-called."

The woman he walked up to was holding a cell phone to her ear when he approached her. She never removed the phone as she replied, "I don't give a flying fuck about what you would be considered! Nor do I give two fucks about who or what you feel. What you need to do is get the fuck out of my face and go do your job, white boy!"

She was always what someone would call hell on wheels. Mean as a desert Diamond Back rattlesnake and as feisty as an African lioness. Still, she was hands down the most stunningly attractive woman in all of San Francisco in Sgt. Dudley's eyes. Her name was Isabella Santana. She was the perfect blend of Colombian beauty with a kiss of Irish. While she spit her verbal venom, Sgt. Dudley admired her breathtaking body of perfection. She stood 5'9" without heels. Her 42DD breast sat high and firm on her chest. She had flat athletic abs that accounted for her 27" waist and made her 44-inch ass appear even bigger than it was. Dudley felt his manhood begin to grow.

"Miss Santana, you really shouldn't walk around with such a nasty attitude and vile language. Someday, someone may prevent such foul language from coming out of such pretty lips." Lips that

Sgt. Dudley would be willing to spend top dollar to feel suck on his cock.

"Bitch! Did you just threaten me?" She boldly took a step forward, getting up in his face. "Mothafucka, I'll—" Whomever she was talking to on the phone cut her off. Isabella listened for a moment before saying, "I don't give a fuck about no witnesses. This mothafucka just threatened me in front of—" She was cut off again. Though she appeared visibly frustrated, the fire and venom was out of her voice as she submissively replied, "Okay, Daddy.... Yes, I'm sorry, Daddy."

Sgt. Dudley took her submission wrongfully as a sign of retreat. He smiled as he grabbed the front of his crotch and openly ran his eyes over her body. They lingered on her tits as her anger had caused her nipples to harden and stick out through the material of her shirt.

"That's right, listen to your Daddy before you say something that might get your little pretty ass in trouble." He said this while still staring openly at her breasts.

Isabella bit down on her bottom lip to hold her composure. She mugged the shit out of the disrespectful pig while listening on the phone. When the call was over, she bobbed her head up and down like a nigga with a look on her face that spoke murder.

"Yeah, we'll see, mothafucka! Look while you can, puto. We will see who has the last mothafuck'n laugh!"

Sgt. Dudley started to respond to her threat but decided against it. He had already allowed his emotions to get the best of him. He wouldn't allow himself to further argue with her as if he was some common, low-life street punk.

When he looked around all eyes were focused on him and Isabella. He boldly returned some of the stares he received from some of the nosey onlookers, before turning his back on the peasants and walking back to the crime scene to do his job.

Thirty feet away, Detective Morgan watched the entire display with a look of utter disdain on her face. She shook her head in disgust as she watched her partner walk away from the tall Hispanic chick.

***

One thing Kino didn't tolerate was disrespect. There was no question about whether he would honor his vow to Isabella. His word was his bond, and he gave her his word that Harry Potter would answer for his disrespect. He didn't give a fuck about Harry Potter being the head of the Gang Task Force. The police bled the same as any other nigga.

For now, though, his attention was needed somewhere else. More pressing matters were at hand.

"What it look like brah, brah?" Stubby asked Kino once he got off the phone.

"Harry Potter and that lil' bitch of his over in the jets doing they lil' routine. While I was talking to Bella, Harry Potter came over to her running his mouth talking real Greezy and shit. I had to calm Bella down and talk her out of getting all up in his shit." Kino picked up his glass of Remy Martin and took a long swallow.

"Blood, I'm getting tired of that white boy. That mothafucka around the hood all day like he can't be touched, with his crooked ass." Secretly, Stubby had his own plans for dealing with Sgt. Dudley. He ain't said nothing to his brothers yet because he felt it wasn't time. But it was getting close.

"Them pigs always planting shit and locking niggaz up on bogus ass charges. That nigga Freak still ain't home. I still can't believe they gave the homie all that time when it was clear as day that the nigga was set up by Harry Potter." Just thinking about the fuck nigga shit that Harry Potter been getting away with had John Dough pissed the fuck off.

"That white mothafucka been running round this bitch like he think he that nigga Denzel in *Training Day*," Baby Shoota voiced.

"Man, fuck that cracker! We'll deal with that shit later. Right now, niggaz need to find out who the fuck them Mexicans was and why the fuck they just unloaded on the Jets." Kino wasn't about to waste time talking about all the crooked shit Harry Potter had been doing and was capable of.

"Brah, I don't give a fuck why they did that shit! The only thing that we need to know is who the fuck were they. Why they did that shit don't matter. Them niggaz did that shit. Now they gotta answer for it." John Dough really couldn't give a fuck about reasons. He couldn't believe some Mexicans had the balls to disrespect the block like they did.

Ordinarily, John Dough was strictly about his money. That's why he got the handle "John Dough." He was chasing the bag so much that people often forgot that he was a straight up beast in his own right.

"My nigga, ain't no question 'bout it. Them niggaz fa'sho gonna answer for that shit. But knowing why the fuck they did it could be important." Kino's level of adrenaline was still elevated due to the shootout.

"Yo, I'm with Dough on this, my nigga. I don't give a fuck why them mothafuckas came thru. All I wanna know is who it was so we can slide on them mothafuckas." Stubby racked back the slide on the choppa he had been wiping down.

"Yo, how we know it wasn't one of them spic bitches? I mean, y'all fucking with them two bitches, then out the blue, these mothafuckas pull that move? Shit don't add up, my nigga." John Dough was never one to bite his tongue, and he damn sure wasn't going to do it now.

"First off, you need to watch your disrespectful ass mouth, nicca. I don't know who the fuck you calling a spic. Ain't nobody up in here disrespecting you, calling you all out of your name and shit, so you don't need to be up in here disrespecting me and my cousin. Second of all, what the fuck would me or Abella have some clowns come shoot up the projects while we were up in there for? Nicca, how stupid does that sound? So, you can miss me with the mothafuck'n conspiracy theories, 'cause we could've died right along with your black ass." Rosalinda had been in the back room trying to calm her cousin Abella down.

She'd never been around anything like the shootout earlier, so Abella was pretty shaken up. Rosalinda didn't like hearing the fucked-up accusations that John Dough was throwing on the table, and she wasn't about to just let the shit slide either.

"Damn, lil' mamma, speak on that shit," Baby Shoota joked. "Let that nigga know 'bout that spicey Latina shit!"

"This ain't the time to be on no bullshit, Dough." Stubby didn't find it funny. This was a time to deal with nothing but real shit.

"Dough, Stubby got a point, my nigga. Rosalinda is good 'cause I vouch for her. That in itself should be good for everybody here. If you're questioning her, my nigga, you're questioning me." Kino could feel his adrenaline slowly creeping back up.

"Kino, ain't nobody questioning you nor your judgment, my nigga. I'm merely overturning every rock possible and throwing every scenario on the table. And, my nigga, considering the circumstances, her setting us up is a plausible scenario." John Dough wasn't trying to cause any friction among them. He was simply stating what he felt was obvious. Plus, he wasn't about to tuck tail for nan nigga. Not even his own nigga.

"Well, my nigga, I'm telling you that shit ain't possible, and we ain't even considering it. Lil' mama's official. That's it and that's all!" Kino started to say something else, but the sound of his cell phone ringing interrupted him.

He grabbed his phone and checked the caller ID. Seeing the name, he answered the call. Hopefully, he'd get some answers. The call was from the older homie, Half Dead. Half Dead was an original head busta from San Francisco's Hunters Point. One of them OGs that was so feared when he was younger that everyone was glad the day he decided to stop running the streets. He still had his hands in a lot of shit. Which kept him connected in some way to almost everybody who was somebody in the city.

Kino listened for a few moments after answering the phone. Everybody sat waiting for the call to end so they could finish their discussion.

"What? OG, you're sure about this shit?" Kino asked Half Dead, not believing the shit he was hearing. "Yeah, alright OG, good looking out, homie. Off top, it's all good, brah."

Straight Beast Mode 2

Kino hung up the phone and looked over at Rosalinda. "Rosa, go on in the back and check on your cousin." She knew better than to question him, especially at a time like this, so she walked back down the hall to the back room.

Once they heard the back room door close, Kino addressed the others. "That was the OG Half Dead. Nigga said supposedly, them mothafuckas were some Norteños from East Palo Alto. They supposed to be linked in with them niggaz from 21st. That nigga Crazy and them."

Kino sat and waited for that shit to register. It was Stubby that said something. "That shit don't make no sense. What the fuck would make them bitches over at 21st Street want to start some shit with us for?"

"The fuck if I know. But you niggaz know just as good as I do that if it's coming from that old nigga Half Dead, then shit gots to be official." Kino looked at all three of them.

"Like a referee's whistle," Baby Shoota said.

"You still fuck wit' that Taliban nigga from PA on that music shit?" Stubby asked Kino.

"Who you talkin' 'bout, that nigga Shark?"

"Shit, I don't remember that crazy ass niggaz name, the nigga that always say that don't let that bother you shit," Stubby told him.

Kino laughed. "Yeah, that's that nigga. I still fucks with blood, and I already know where you're going. I'mma hit that nigga up and see what's good. See what that nigga know 'bout them mothafuckas Half Dead talking 'bout."

Stubby stood up with the choppa in his hands. "First, let's ride and see what these 21st Street bitches talking 'bout."

"Nigga, you already know." John Dough stood up.

"What's understood ain't gotta be said." Baby Shoota was always ready for that gunplay.

"I'll meet y'all niggaz outside." Kino stood up and walked to the back room while everybody else made their way out of the house.

After the shooting they all had to get off Sunnydale. So, they rode over to Rosalinda's spot not too far off. This wasn't the first time niggaz had to duck off at Isabella's spot.

Kino knocked on the door to the back room. A few moments later Rosalinda opened the door. When she saw it was Kino, she stepped out into the hallway and closed the room door softly behind her.

"How's she doing?" he asked her.

"She's okay. She finally was able to calm down enough to go to sleep a while ago. She was sleep when I came out not too long ago."

"How are you doing"

She put her hands on hips. "Are you sure you should be back here fraternizing with the enemy?"

He reached his arms out and wrapped them around her, pulling her a step closer to him. He looked her in her eyes. Kino could see that she wasn't really hurt, yet he decided to confront her anyway, softly telling her, "Don't trip off that shit that Dough said. You know he was just on edge behind that bullshit. As much as you've rocked for us, you know ain't none of the team gonna question your loyalty."

"It's not fair, Kino. I already have to share you with other women. I shouldn't have to deal with any added bullshit on top of that." Kino loved when she pouted. She looked so sexy when she did. She knew it too.

He kissed her softly on her lips, sucking on the bottom one for a little bit when he was done. "Look, we just got the line on something, so we gotta take off. But me and you gonna finish this when I'm done."

"Oh, so you're coming back?" Rosalinda leaned forward, stealing a kiss of her own.

"You can bet that nice pretty little ass of yours I'm coming back so I can fuck the life out of you."

"Mmmm, you better." One more kiss, then she let him go. Though he didn't say it, she knew what he had to go do.

Straight Beast Mode 2

Kino walked down the hall with a hard dick, promising himself that he was coming back for some of Rosalinda's fire pussy.

De'Kari

Chapter 7

Mission St. was one of San Francisco's main streets. It was one of those streets that buzzed with activity twenty-four hours a day. A street that never sleeps. All up and down its long street illegal activity was operational out in the open as if it were legal. Mission was a sort of Skid Row where someone could come looking for almost any low-life thing imaginable. Everything from drugs and guns to sex and slaves could be found and purchased somewhere on Mission St. Walking down the street and seeing someone openly shooting dope up their arms was just as natural as finding a liquor store on the corner in the hood.

The blocks and blocks of people that crowded Mission Street didn't mean a mothafuck'n thing to the four niggaz in the older model Nissan Pathfinder. Its occupants hungrily searched the sidewalk for any potential victims. Most of the people they saw were junkies, wandering the streets lost. Zombies looking for nothing particular yet searching for whatever.

They were stuck slowly moving behind a beat-up old Lincoln Continental. It had a bumper sticker on the right bumper. It read, *If you don't like my driving, you can KISS MY ASS!*

Another sticker on the left said, *Honk your horn if I'm driving too slow... BITCH!*

John Dough liked the bumper stickers. He smiled to himself as he sat behind the wheel of the Pathfinder. That was some shit he'd probably put on his own bumper.

"There we go right there!" Baby Shoota got excited when he saw the four Mexicans huddled together next to Issa's Liquors. The group looked to be in the middle of a drug transaction.

The one standing in the middle of the group had his head down. He was looking down at something he was holding in his hands. The guy standing in front of him had his back to the direction the Pathfinder was. His head was down looking at whatever it was the first guy was looking at. The third Mexican, the one standing to the left of the one in the middle, was staring at exactly the same thing as the first two.

The only one who seemed not to be interested in what everyone else was looking at was the fourth man. The one standing off to the right. His right arm was in the pocket of his jacket giving off the impression that he was holding something. His head swiveled back and forth right and left while his eyes scanned any and everything he saw.

The four inside the truck were up and game. They knew exactly what was going on. Drug sales were as natural and occurrence in the street life as neighborhood watch was in middle suburbia.

"Shoota, you and Stubby already know what time it is," Kino spoke as he reached for the handle of the front passenger side door.

"Nigga, say less." Baby Shoota called over his shoulder. He was already exiting the truck.

Without any other words being spoken among them, they moved with an individualized precision. One that betrayed their many years doing drills with each other. Baby Shooter was a few feet in front of Kino off to his right. He held his cell phone in his left hand and appeared to be scrolling through his phone in search for something as he walked.

As Baby Shoota walked past the group that was huddled together near the store, the Mexican with his hand in his pocket eyed him suspiciously. Baby Shoota could feel the eyes of the cold stare on him. Yet he walked on by as if he had no clue he was being watched. The lookout needed to stay alert. At the moment he didn't detect any hostile or weird vibes coming from Baby Shoota. He focused his attention to the block.

He was just in time to see a bright yellow-skinned Snoop Doggy Dogg looking mothafucka walking up to them with a knot of money in his hands. He was fumbling with the money. looking for the right denominations. The hairs on the back of the neck of the lookout stood up instantly. He could feel all sorts of vibes coming off the ghetto Snoop Dogg. They all were the wrong kind of vibes. The ones that put niggaz on alert.

"Aye, say, my nigga, I need a fifty-piece. One of you niggaz hook ya boi up?" Kino separated the correct bills from the rest and put the remainder of the wad in his pocket.

The lookout didn't have time to wonder what it was that threw him off about the nigga. It was time to act not think. He stepped forward while putting his free hand out to block Kino's path. "Whoa! Homie! You gotta hold up. You can't just come barging all up on mothafuckas like you crazy or something. Can't you see—" He couldn't finish his sentence because his thoughts were blown out of his head by the bullet Baby Shoota put in that mothafucka.

The loud sound of the gunshot rang out through the night. The back of the lookout's brains along with his thoughts were sprayed on the wall. His body jerked from the force of the bullet before crumbling like a used, wet Kleenex. Only then did the second lookout, who'd been more interested in the transaction than he was looking out, look up to see what was going on.

The tweaker that was there to score some more crystal stood shaking visibly from head to toe with a bewildered look on his face. He didn't know what to do. He was so spun his mind couldn't slow down enough for him to make a single rational decision. Run, stay, hide, scream, cry, beg for his life. These along with a million other thoughts ran through his mind simultaneously. Causing his mind to go into overdrive. All he could do was stand there and tremble in fear.

The Mexican who was in the middle holding the sack of dope that they were all focused on was seventeen years old and had only been jumped into the gang six days ago. Being a bag holder was his first official assignment for the 21st Norteños Gang. Unfortunately, it would be his last.

He stood in utter disbelief as the warm, slimy liquid that was blood and brain matter ran down his face. When the lookout stepped up to block Kino's path, he had actually stepped within a foot of the seventeen-year-old wannabe. A third of the blood and brain matter that flew out of the back of the lookout's head spread across the kid's face.

In a state of utter shock, the kid just stood there holding the bag of dope pissing on himself. For no apparent reason he stuck his tongue out and licked his lips. They were covered in the warm, thick substance. The taste was a salty, coppery-like taste. Just as it began to register in his mind what he was licking, Kino, who had shoved the wad of money into the pocket of his hooded sweatshirt, pulled his hand back out of the pocket. It was now holding a black Glock 27, which Kino placed directly under the kid's chin. The kid's head snapped back so hard from the force of the gunshot when Kino pulled the trigger that it snapped his brain stem. He died instantly.

Some pedestrians screamed and yelled while running, trying to get away from the gruesome murders. Others simply walked and continued on about their business as if nothing happened. These were the ones who'd long since grown accustomed to the violent kill or be killed way of life inside of the urban jungle known as San Francisco.

The third Mexican was a little smarter and scarier than his comrades. When Baby Shoota blew the back of the lookout's head off and he looked up and saw his friend's body falling, he didn't freeze up like the others. Instead, he took off like a quarter horse fresh out of the gates. The only protection with that was he ran in the wrong direction.

He was too busy looking behind him, as if he expected to find the Boogey Man chasing him, to see where he was going. Too distracted to see John Dough before he ran into him.

"What's up, homie, you alright?" John Dough played the concerned citizen worried about the Mexican who'd just crashed into him.

"M-m-move, dumb ass!" The frightened Mexican tried to push John Dough out of his way.

A look of surprise came on his face as he felt a violent, hot, piercing pain tear into his chest. It was followed by another. Then another. The loud thunderous roar that accompanied every fresh stabbing pain was like the voice of God in his ears. Cursing him, his judgment for all the fucked-up things he'd done in life.

Everything happened so fast. Yet time seemed to slow down to nanoseconds inside what was left of the lookout's mind. As his semi-lifeless eyes took in the shattered visualization of everything that had just played out in front of his eyes. It all happened as his body was crumbling to the pavement.

His eyes involuntarily blinked when what was left of his head bounced off of the sidewalk. As the pair of brand-new Nike Foamposites crossed his line of sight, that's when it finally registered why the Snoop Dogg lookalike alarmed him. No dope fiend would be wearing a pair of brand-new Nike Foamposites. The last of his thoughts ran out onto the concrete with what was left of his brain. The last image to register in his dying mind was the Foamposites climbing inside of an SUV that suddenly stopped before speeding away.

De'Kari

Chapter 8

There was a heavy law enforcement presence present at the Mark Zuckerberg General Hospital. Niggaz in San Francisco didn't believe in or give a fuck about a so-called neutral zone. That shit didn't exist in Frisco. Because of that mentality shoot outs and fights were common at the hospital, which was the reason for the heavy police presence. Locals always joked that changing the name was the city's futile attempt at trying to sweep the hospital's violent reputation under a translucent rug. To true Frisconians the hospital would always be San Francisco General.

Lil' Dooka wasn't worried about the police, and neither was Nardy. They both had their bangers on them as they walked through the sliding entrance doors of the hospital. Right now, the Devil himself wouldn't bother the two young killers. One look at the two stone-cold faces would tell anyone to back the fuck up!

The hospital was crowded and noisy. The heart-piercing screams and cries of young mothers, sisters, and spouses who were being delivered the tragic news that their loved ones didn't or wouldn't make it, haunted the hallways like evil spirits that haunt the minds of psychotics.

Lil' Dooka couldn't believe how much shit happened over something so small as a bitch getting her ass grabbed. It didn't make no fucking sense. None whatsoever! He'd lost his brothers, his heart. Aunt Dee laid buried inside the cold, hard ground of the cemetery. Now MoMo and TG lay up in the hospital fighting for their lives.

MoMo was the lucky one. According to his doctor there was so much cocaine and alcohol in his system when he got shot that his body refused to shut down even though it should've. The cocaine kept his system on overdrive, which saved his young life. The doctor went so far as to say that in his professional opinion, there was so much cocaine inside of MoMo's system that he seriously doubted if MoMo had felt any pain at all.

TG, on the other hand, wasn't so lucky. The three 40-caliber bullets that violently invaded his chest nearly took his life. No one could offer any sort of conclusive professional explanation as to why he was alive. One of the bullets sliced through his aorta, nearly severing it. This alone was enough to kill most people. The second bullet that hit vertical to his chest caused his left lung to collapse, making him need the assistance of a breathing machine to keep oxygen flowing into his body. The third and fourth bullets caused damage as well, just not to any vital organs like the first two had done. One bullet shattered his collar bone when it crashed into it while the other hit his chest with so much force, that it cracked his sternum, the plate that covered a person's chest.

The doctors didn't know whether TG was going to make it or not. The only thing the doctor could say for sure was TG was fighting an uphill battle, and the odds were not in the young man's corner.

"Dooka? Dooka?" Nardy looked at Lil' Dooka with a mug on his face because Lil' Dooka was ignoring him.

Shaking his head, snapping out of his thoughts, Lil' Dooka replied, "Huh? My bad, Nardy, what's up?"

"Man, you throwing me off, Dooka. Nigga, this shit is getting really heavy and you spacing out on niggaz. You throwing me off." Nardy was scared. Too much was going on, but he couldn't show his fear. He refused to make Lil' Dooka think he was soft. But the truth was he was ready to throw in the towel and squash the beef.

"What? You sound stupid, brah. Nigga, I'm not spacing out, fuck you mean, brah! I was just going over some shit in my head. Figuring out our next play. Them sucka side niggaz acting like they 'bout this life when them niggaz is really bitches. Nigga, on BR, I gotta come up with something that'll show these pussies that this shit ain't a game." Lil' Dooka had never been more serious about anything in his life.

They paused in front of the elevator. Nardy pushed the button to call the elevator. "Dooka that's the shit I'm talking about. You sitting here talking about you gotta do this, and you gotta do that like you the only one out here. Dooka you been acting like it's you against the world nigga like we ain't all involved in this shit. We was supposed to be getting money Dooka not losing each other over some stupid shit. You been throwing me off ever since Budda been gone."

Lil' Dooka cut Nardy off. "Look Nord it's too late to be tripping off of what the fuck it's all behind. Nigga them niggaz done spilled blood now this shit ain't gonna end until all them niggaz is dead. As far as Budda leaving, nigga somebody had to step up, so I did. That's the only thing that changed." The elevator arrived, making Lil' Dooka cut his sentence short. Wasn't no telling who was behind the doors.

When the elevator doors opened a young Middle Eastern couple walked off of the elevator. Two niggaz and a sistah who looked to bin her thirties stayed on the elevator. Nardy stepped into the elevator first followed by Lil' Dooka. The tension between the four men was felt immediately once the elevator doors closed. After pushing the button for the correct floor Nardy stood with his back against the wall and his hands by his waistline inches away from the Glock.

The sistah noticed his behavior and looked Nardy in his eyes. At least she tried to. She couldn't because Nardy, whom she was positive she had never seen before in her life was eyeballing her little brother like he wanted to kill him. She looked over at her little brother and couldn't believe he was doing the same thing. This puzzled her because her little brother wouldn't harm a fly.

Lil' Dooka saw the way the bitch looked between Nardy and the sucka that was in front of him on the other side of the elevator. But he paid the bitch no mind. His focus really was on the nigga in front of him.

When the Middle Eastern couple stepped off the elevator the nigga in front of him was initially standing where Lil' Dooka was now. When he saw Nardy and Lil' Dooka the nigga stepped across the elevator to the same side the other nigga was standing on. The bitch was all the way at the back in the middle of the elevator. Looking at the four of them.

The older of the two niggaz, the one standing in front of Lil' Dooka looked like the New York rapper DMX except he had a long scar running down the side of his face. Seeing Nardy's hand rest on the Medusa head of his Versace jeans. He put his hand inside of the pocket in front of his hoodie. He gave his head a very slight nod as if he was asking Lil' Dooka "What's up?"

The sistah who happened to be his fiancé saw this gesture too and flipped the fuck out. "You mothafuckas got to be out y'all rabid ass minds if y'all think some shit is about to pop off in this mothafuckas!" She turned her attention to the nigga with the scar on his face. "DeAndre don't act like yo ass don't hear me! My baby is in here fighting for her life and yo ass is ready to get into a shootout with two little boys in this mothafuck'n elevator! Whatever the fuck the problem you have with these two little niggaz cannot be more important than yo daughter needing her father. Now you need to take yo mothafuck'n hand off of that gun and out of that pocket before you fuck around and have me lose my fucking religion!"

The elevator stopped and the doors opened. Outside the elevator a young black couple was waiting to get on the elevator. The young man took one look inside of the elevator, accessed the situation and made a quick decision.

"Shit, fuck that. We gonna take the mothafuck'n stairs. Come on bitch!" He grabbed the woman that was with him and quickly walked off.

The elevator doors closed again and continued its rise. The nigga in front of Lil' Dooka with the scar on his face was the one the woman called DeAndre. Both pain and anger could easily be seen in his eyes. A lot of pain and even more anger. He was so angry about his daughter being shot by a stray bullet, that he was ready to take his pain and anger out on anybody. However, after his baby mama's words. He rationalized that now was not the time nor the place.

As he smiled within, DeAndre removed his hand from the butt of the compact Glock and took his hand out of his pocket. The two little niggaz could thank God for his baby mama cause the bitch just saved their lives.

The elevator stopped on their floor, DeAndre, his bitch, and her brother all got off of the elevator. As they got off, Lil' Dooka was silently thinking the same thoughts as DeAndre. Only in Lil'

Straight Beast Mode 2

Dooka's mind it was them that God saved them, the two-pussy ass niggaz and that ugly man looking black bitch.

Nardy was just glad that shit didn't escalate any further than it had done. He was smart enough to realize that if they had started shooting inside of the little ass elevator, the chances were that they all would have been fucked up. All four of them. As the doors were closing Nardy realized that they were on the floor that TG was on. He caught the doors and told Lil' Dooka that he was going to check on TG and would meet Lil' Dooka at MoMo's room when his was done.

Lil' Dooka was glad that Nardy decided to swing by TG's room. Nardy was starting to get on his mothafuck'n nerves with all of his mothafuck'n crying. He could tell that Nardy blamed him for everything. Everybody did. Lil' Dooka could see it in everybody's eyes. Mothafuckas all acted like all this shit was his fault. Like he was the one who had grabbed the little bitch ass that night at the function.

When the doors to the elevator opened Lil' Dooka walked off the elevator with his mind made up that if he ever seen the nigga with the scar on his face again. He was going to kill him. He wasn't stupid he knew all of his frustrations was with his own niggaz. But the name of the game was fuck the other side which meant that they took everything out on everybody else. They never brought harm to each other. Since he couldn't do anything to Nardy, the nigga with the scar on his face just made himself a target. That's just how it was.

Lil' Dooka was halfway down the hall from MoMo's room when the door leading to MoMo's room opened up. The sexiest little white bitch he had ever seen came walking out of the room. She was a little bitch, stacked like she was from Georgia or some mothafuck'n where. Her body could have easily cost twenty-something thousand dollars. Yet the way she carried it under her nurse uniform Lil' Dooka could tell that shit was all hers.

She just so happened to come his way. Lil' Dooka couldn't help but thin to himself that she walked like she would really put a hurting on a niggaz dick. He bit down on his bottom lip while undressing her with his eyes. The contrast of dark blue and red colors of her hair against her pale skin was enough to spark all kinds of wild sexual fantasies in Lil' Dooka's mind.

When they got to within feet of each other, the feelings changed. Something about the bitch sent alarms through his body. All sorts of bells and whistles began going off inside of his mind. As they pass by each other the two of them made eye contact. A cold chilling jolt of electricity traveled the waves of Lil' Dooka's nerves. Without realizing it, his had moved closer to the Glock that was on his waist. He didn't know if he wanted to fuck her brains out or to blow them out her mothafuck'n head. This threw him off.

When she smiled at him the hairs on the back of Lil' Dooka's neck stood up. In that brief second when she smiled at him. She let her guard down and he got a glimpse at how dangerous the beautiful little white bitch was. The moment passed just as quickly as their bodies passed one another.

Lil' Dooka couldn't shake the feeling that came over him. How could a little mothafuckas that sexy have such violent and deadly eyes? Just as he reached the door to MoMo's room, he heard some sort of alarm going off the nurse's station. He paused to look over his shoulder for another look at the little white bitch. He was just in time to see her walk onto the elevator.

"Excuse me sir!" A nurse called out from behind him.

He turned around to see who the fuck had the balls to put their hands on him. A group of nurses was behind the one who'd pushed him out of the way. They were all frantically rushing inside of MoMo's room. He followed them inside.

"I am sorry sir, but I am going to have to ask you to wait out in the hallway." A young Filipino nurse in a pair of green scrubs put her arm out across his chest. Blocking his path into the room.

"Bitch you sound dumb as fuck. That's my brother over there. I'm not going nowhere." Lil' Dooka didn't know why he was suddenly overcome with fear.

"I am sorry sir but right now there are complications, and we can't allow you to be in here until things are back under control."

"W-what? What are you talking 'bout? Bitch, what's wrong with my brother?"

"Sir" was all she could get out before Lil' Dooka pushed her out of his way.

A buff ass male Nigerian stepped in Lil' Dooka's way. He looked at Lil' Dooka like he was daring him to try and push him out of the way.

"Oh nigga, you think this is a game or something?" Lil' Dooka reached under his shirt. Grabbing the handle of the Glock that was on his waist.

As he was starting to pull the Glock off of his waist. A strong hand gripped his waist preventing him from pulling the Glock free. Lil' Dooka looked down first at the hand that seized him. Then he turned his head to the right so he could look into the eyes of a dead man.

All anger and hostility melted away immediately upon looking into the eyes of the nigga who'd grabbed his wrist.

De'Kari

Chapter 9

Lil' Dooka looked up from the hand that grabbed his wrist ready to kill somebody. With his nose flared and teethed bared ready for whatever. He looked up into the eyes of the one man whom he both loved and respected above all.

"Let me find out yo' ass was 'bout to whip out right the fuck in this room and catch a body." Budda had a smirk on his face and humor in his voice. Yet the seriousness he was feeling was evident in his eyes.

"W-what…H-how…" So many questions were running through Lil' Dooka's mind, he could form the words to verbally formulate the questions that were in his mind into words.

"Yeah, yeah, whatever nigga. Come outside so these people can do their thang with brah. We can holla out there nigga" The alarms and bells were still going off while the nurse and a doctor tended to MoMo.

The buff Nigerian didn't know who the Asian looking an was who stopped the kid from pulling out what he knew in his heart was a gun. He silently thanked God for sending whoever the guy was.

"Body is going into anabolic shock; we need to get this young man to the operating room STAT! Call Dr. Elabed and tell him I need him in operating room A-3 for immediate operation."

Lil' Dooka didn't hear the last of the doctors' orders because the room door was closed behind him. He closed his eyes and took a deep breath forcing back the tears that threatened to escape his eyelids. Thoughts of the day they lost BR entered his mind.

Something woke him out of his sleep. He didn't know what had disturbed his sleep until he rolled over and noticed the door to his cell was open. The little homie Miles, from Excelsior was standing in the open doorway.

"Bitch let me find out you was 'bout to try some 1980's American me shit on the kid. Trynna take the kid cheeks while I'm sleeping and shit." Lil' Dooka joked.

Miles didn't laugh. Instead, he had a fucked up look on his face. He lowered his head and mumbled something that Lil' Dooka couldn't make out. It couldn't have been no later than seven o'clock in the morning. Miles was out because he was the pod worker for the day. Lil' Dooka asked him to repeat whatever he just said.

"MoMo *got shot last night. He got hit in the head and his brother was killed."*

Lil' Dooka's heart fell out of his chest. His world stopped. "Bitch stop playing! Brah you know we don't play them kind of games."

"Dooka, I'm not playing brah they were driving on eighty last night when somebody started shoot...." *He never heard the rest. Lil' Dooka jumped off of his top bunk.*

As he did, Deputy Ovalle's voice came over the intercom in his cell, "Jordan this is Ovalle, come to the Deputy's Station."

By the time Lil' Dooka made it out of his cell, his face was drenched in tears. As Ovalle confirmed the news his mind was still in denial. That denial lasted as he made his way to the wall phones. It was like living inside of a lucid nightmare.

Lil' Dooka didn't even realize he had dialed his mom's number until her voice came over the line, "Hello Baby."

"Tell me it ain't true Mama, tell me it ain't true." *He pleaded with her. Needing it to be a lie. A sick joke or even perhaps, somehow a terrible mistake.*

"DeAndre, I'm sorry baby it's true. MoMo was shot in his head and Nina's son Baby Reno was killed...."

Right there in 5-West, Lil' Dooka held the phone in silence. Stunned. The tears didn't fall, they flowed in torrents out of his eyes.

Out in the hallway Lil' Dooka blinked back tears again. He knew he had to remain strong, he just didn't know how. Hell, he was a young adult. Only a few years ago they were innocent kids going to Balboa Highschool. Now death followed them like some sort of sadistic chaperone.

He was about to open his mouth to say something to Budda. Before he got a chance to, the door to MoMo's room was snatched open. Nurses and the two doctors flew by with MoMo on a gurney and raced off down the hallway headed toward the operating room.

Straight Beast Mode 2

That's when it hit Lil' Dooka like a punch from Iron Mike Tyson. The white bitch!

He bolted down the hallway in the opposite direction the nurses and doctors went. Lil' Dooka ran full speed in the direction of the elevators. That strange lethal feeling that he saw in them pretty emerald, green eyes. He still didn't understand why, but he just knew that the white bitch in the nurse's uniform had something to do with whatever the fuck just happened to MoMo.

Budda didn't hesitate to think or try to make any sense out of what was going on. His instincts were screaming at him, and he listened to them bitches. He took off right behind Lil' Dooka!

Following Lil' Dooka, they ran right pass the elevators and crashed through the door leading to the stairs. They raced down the stairs two, sometimes three steps at a time. Everyone was alarmed and frightened as the two men burst out of the bottom stairway into the first-floor lobby with guns in their hands.

In a very dramatic way, some bitch in the background screamed like she was being attacked, neither Budda nor Lil' Dooka paid the stupid bitch any attention. They ignored her like they ignored the alarmed looks on the faces of the security guards they raced pass on their way out of the hospital doors.

Out in the hospital parking lot, Lil' Dooka stopped running. He was breathing heavy as he concentrated. Eyes scanning the parking lot for any sign of the beautiful little She-Devil. He had to find her. He couldn't let the bitch get away!

His eyes scanned left then right. Then left again. Desperately searching the parking lot, parked cars, moving vehicles. Anywhere. Everywhere. All at once. All the while breathing like a maniac. A raging bull.

He couldn't find her. With all of his energy everything that made him, him. He searched.

Budda could feel people staring at them as they stood there in search for what, he didn't know. He looked around and only saw the faces that belonged to the eyes of the people staring at them like they were crazy. He silently hoped Lil' Dooka hadn't done just that. Hoped his little brother hadn't finally succumbed to the extreme pressures that were stacked on his shoulders and finally lost his mind.

Budda heard Lil' Dooka let out a long deep breath before he slumped his shoulders in defeat and tucked his Glock back under his shirt, on his waist.

"Uh...Is everything okay fellas?" Both Budda and Lil' Dooka turned to face the security guard that asked them the question.

As he was doing so, something caught Lil' Dooka's eye. He quickly turned his attention back to whatever it was. His hand instantly went back to his waist and gripped his cannon. It was the sun's light that just happened to bounce off of the glass of freshly polished and waxed candy-painted taffy blue Lincoln Navigator. The truck itself was turning out of the parking lot onto the street. When it turned long, cherry red hair blew out of the window and flowed in the wind. The electric jolt that he felt in the pit of his stomach told him that it was her. He felt the conviction down in his bones.

There was no need to pull the Glock out, Lil' Dooka knew that they were too far away. The truck was seconds away from disappearing. Just before it did, as if she could sense that they had come out of the hospital and was standing in the parking lot gawking at her. She turned her head in their direction. For the briefest of seconds made eye contact. Instead of smiling, she blew him a kiss and pulled off.

Budda had no idea who the white bitch in the Navigator was, but his instincts told him she was the reason they rushed out of the hospital. "Who the fuck is the bitch, Dook?" he asked Lil' Dooka as they both watched the truck disappear.

"Fuck!" The frustration was clearly etched on Lil' Dooka's face. For the second time his head fell away from his waist.

Not a moment too soon either. Two uniformed SFPD officers came cautiously walking up to them. They addressed the security guards.

"Everything okay fellas?" The older of the two officers directed the question at the security guards but was eyeing Budda and Lil' Dooka.

"U-uh... y-yes fellas everything's okay." The security guard grew up in Hunters Point. He was some disillusioned fool who thought he was on the same side as the cops. He knew to the cops he was still a nigga.

The second eyed Lil' Dooka real suspiciously. "Are you sure about that?" he asked. Hoping he received an answer that would justify him adding one more figure to the number of black men killed by law enforcement.

Picking up on the cops undertone. Budda let both of his hands rest right next to the two F's on his Fendi belt buckle. In front of the twin Glock 30's that were tucked in his waist. "You can always act like it ain't if you want to. Bet you'll never see Trump Make America Great again!" Them being cops didn't mean shit to Budda. If this racist mothafuckas wanted it Budda would gladly give him everything he asked for.

The security guard took a step in between Budda and the racist cop.

"Uh.... As I said fellas everything is okay out here. We do not need your assistance." At 6'3" and 260lbs the security guard had a commanding presence.

The first cop, the older of the two, thought about something for a moment before looking around and seeing all the faces of the people watching them. Some of the people actually had their phones out and were recording them.

"It's alright Gillispie. These guys say they got everything under control out here. Let's say we head back over to the station early and get some paperwork out the way." He'd had enough years of experience to know when to leave well enough alone.

Gillispie looked as if he wanted to say something else with his racist pink faced ass. Instead, he turned around and steamed off. Mumbling under his breath like the little bitch he was.

"Fucking faggot." Lil' Dooka couldn't help himself.

He filled Budda in on the shit with the white bitch as they made their way back inside of the hospital. When he was done Budda fully understood why Lil' Dooka felt the way he did about the white bitch he saw with the Harley Quinn hairdo.

Budda was the first of the two off the elevator. Lil' Dooka was busy checking a text message he just got from Gabby. Lil' Dooka was saying something, but Budda wasn't listening. He was focused on Nardy who was standing in front of MoMo's room with the little nurse that had asked Lil' Dooka to step out of the room. They were almost fifteen feet away, yet their body language spoke loud enough for Budda to know something was wrong. Nardy was standing with his back slightly bowed. His head was down like he was looking at his shoes. He was slowly shaking his head. She stood a couple of feet in front of him off to the side. One hand was on Nardy's shoulder, more so in a comforting way instead of a flirtatious one. The arm was slightly bent, and she appeared to be speaking in a hushed tone. Budda already knew what time it was.

"Did you hear me nigga? I said I'm about to be a Daddy, Gabby just sent me a message saying she is pregnant?" Lil' Dooka was responding to the text he just read as he spoke.

"Congratulation's nigga" Budda responded. Then he mumbled to himself. "A life for a life. One life is taken, while another one is given."

This caused Lil' Dooka to look up. By now they were a few feet away. When he saw Nardy and the nurse, Lil' Dooka saw the tears running down Nardy's face. An ice-cold arctic chill washed over his body. His cell phone slipped out his hands. Cracking the screen as it hit the floor.

Chapter 10

"Uh...Ugh... ooh shit! Yeah. Right there nigga! Right mothafuck'n there! Fuck this pussy nigga!"

The headboard sounded like gunshots as it banged repeatedly up against the wall of the bedroom.

"Harder, Murda! Fuck this pussy, Daddy! Ooooh, yes, oh my gaawd." Kia's loud cries of passion had C1ty's dick rock hard. She was loud as she talked that shit. "Come on... give me that dick...uh...ungh...uh...ooh shit. Yes, Daddy, yes!"

As loud as she was, Kia wasn't what woke C1ty. It was the sound of his cell phone. Ignoring Kia and her porn performance. He adjusted his dick inside of his pants and reached for his phone. He knew it was G-Baby because of the ring tone.

He answered without hesitation. "Mmmm.... what's up, baby?"

"Don't even try it!" He could tell she had one helluva attitude.

"Don't try what?"

"Don't sweet talk me!"

"And why not?" The sound of the bed banging against the wall was ridiculously loud now.

"It is after three something in the morning De'Mario. Where are you at? Or better yet why ain't you here at home with me? Do you know how many times I done called this damn phone?"

"My bad, baby. I had some stuff to handle with Murda. We were drinking and smoked a little and I must've fell asleep on the couch Babe.

"Oh my God...oh my God...Oh my God! Fuck me Murda! Fuck me! I'mma bout to ...oh shit... oh shit.... Yes Daddy... I'mma cum Daddy!"

"De'Mario what the fuck is that! Nigga you out fucking some stank bitches while I'm here worried sick about yo black ass!"

He couldn't help himself. The shit was fucking hilarious. Before he could stop himself, he started laughing hard as fuck.

"Oh nigga, you think something's funny!?" She sounded like she was ready to jump through the phone and get all up in his ass.

"Woman now you know Doja Cat herself couldn't get me to ever defile my love for you or give away what belongs to you. So yeah, that shit funny. I guess when I fell asleep, him and his chick went back there to do their thang." He still chuckled at how silly G-Baby sounded.

"Boy you better get yo ass home right now so I can do my thang." Sweet seduction replaced the hostility that was just in her voice.

"I'm on my way." He stood up. Grabbing his still hard dick.

"Don't play with me De'Mario."

"I'm not, I'm leaving right now." He hung up the phone still laughing to himself. G-Baby knew exactly how he felt about her. He would never cheat on his baby. She meant everything to him.

He got up and took a piss to release some of the built-up pressure that was on his throbbing dick. He didn't hear Kia anymore, so he figured that round was over at least. On his way out, he shot Murda a message so he wouldn't think that he was still in the front room and not come out to lock shit up.

On the ride home, C1ty's mind wouldn't let him be. It raced a hundred miles an hour. He missed his brother like crazy. No matter what he tried to tell himself about life and death. Acceptance of the loss of Wes was a pill that just was too much to swallow.

This beef they had going on with the Tre-4 niggaz was quickly becoming a major thorn in the side of their plans. C1ty had to remind himself that it was his responsibility to ensure they didn't allow themselves to become so engrossed in this other shit, that they lost track of or forgot their original goal. They needed to get their heads back in the game and C1ty vowed to do just that.

When he walked into his bedroom, G-Baby was lying in bed with the covers pulled back. She was completely naked. He could tell by how much she was glistening between her thighs, that she had begun without him. The heaviness of her eyelids and the allure of her inviting stare were more signs that she was ready to devour him.

Even though he wanted to rush getting undressed. He took his time. Holding her gaze as he removed each article of clothing. Their eyes engaged in an erotic, tantalizing dance of arousal. He made a vow to himself, a silent oath that he was going to beat the brakes off that ass tonight.

Just before he climbed on top of the bed, to make good on his promise. He silently thanked God that she was his and no one else's as he was looking down at her perfection. Seeing her at that moment, he realized why Adam disobeyed God in the Garden of Eden. As an intense flame ignited between their bodies the moment their lips connected.

***

It literally seemed like as soon as C1ty closed his eyes. The early morning socked him right on the chin.

It was his plan to put it down like only he could. Instead, it was G-Baby who ended up putting him down. He smiled as he stretched his slim frame. Replaying in his mind some of the things she had done.

All of the intensity of their multiple rounds, plus all the weed and alcohol C1ty had consumed while he was fucking with Murda, left his body in dire need of some fluids. When he reached the kitchen, G-Baby was at the stove finishing up the breakfast she was making. He walked to the refrigerator and grabbed a bottle of apple juice. G-Baby caught a glimpse of his long dick swinging back and forth as he walked his naked body across the kitchen and smiled.

The cool apple juice tasted like Heaven as it washed down his dry throat. He downed half the bottle then walked over to the stove and wrapped his arm around G-Baby's waist.

"Good morning, Mama." He leaned in and tried to give her a kiss.

It fucked him up when she leaned away from him. "Oh, hell no! I'm sorry, baby, but I know you don't think I'm about to be kissing you with that desert hot breath you got."

"Damn, where the love at?" He feigned like he was hurt.

"The love is in the bathroom on top of the counter baby. It's called *Colgate Advanced White*." She laughed as she teased him.

When he tried to lean in a second time, she dodged his hot lips and lightly smacked him on his ass with the spatula she was using to scramble the eggs.

"Aww shit." C1ty jumped out of shock, not pain. "Okay keep playing. You know I'm all for that kinky shit. Mess around and I'll be eating them eggs off of all this ass while I'm spanking you." for emphasis he reached down and squeezed her ass playfully. Loving how it felt through her panties.

"Boy bye. You and I both know you're not trying to get nothing started. You haven't even recovered yet from that good dose I gave you when got home." She playfully pushed him away.

G-Baby couldn't help laughing when she looked at him to watch him walk out. The spatula had left a grease print on his narrow ass along with a few pieces of scrambled eggs.

Ten minutes later they were both seated at the table eating breakfast. She tried her hardest not to stare. It was hard. The shit he was doing could be called eating in no way, shape, form, or fashion. She had only taken two or three bites and his entire plate was almost gone. He resembled more of an animal eating a fresh kill than he did a human eating breakfast. And he was smacking so loud, it sounded like he was clapping with his mouth.

"You do know that if you choke, I'm not giving you C.P.R. Not with all of that grease and leftovers you got all over your face." She teased.

This got his attention. He was in the middle of biting a piece of turkey sausage when she spoke. He froze. Only then realizing the damage he had done to his plate. He thoughtfully slowed down and chewed the rest of the food in his mouth.

"My bad Mama." C1ty reached for a napkin and wiped his mouth. "A nigga felt like a lone wolf that hadn't eaten in three weeks."

"Shit, you wonder why the pack left. Yo ass ain't leave no food for the rest of the pack." They both laughed at this.

"Genesis, baby, listen." C1ty got serious. He put the napkin down and looked her in her eyes. "I know shit has gotten a little crazy. I need for you to know that I won't let nothing us off course or prevent us from doing what we initially set out to do. The shit that's going down with these Sunnydale niggaz, it is what it is. But it ain't bout to hold us back or hinder us in anyway. Don't think that means that I'mma bout to let them niggaz get away with their disrespect because I'm not. I just have to put my personal feelings aside and think of the entire family. As your man, I had no choice but to show you how much you mean to me by defending your honor. As the head of this family, I have to keep everybody on point."

"De'Mario, baby, you know I know how the game goes. I know you love me without a shadow of doubt. I know why you did what you did, Daddy, because I know you. Just as I know what you have to do for Wes. Baby, all I'm asking is that you make sure that you make it back to me and you don't get lost on the way."

C1ty's cell phone started ringing. He looked at the caller ID and saw that it was Dell. He pressed ignore. And sat the phone back down. His brother would have to wait until their conversation was finished.

"You ain't gotta worry about none of that. They ain't invented a force yet that's strong enough to keep me away from you." his phone started ringing again.

"Well then I suggest you better answer your phone and tell whatever little tramp that is calling that she better learn not to call your phone before one o'clock and then you won't have to worry about ignoring her call." She said as she reached for the jelly to put it on her biscuit.

It was his brother again. He decided to answer the call this time.

"I see you got jokes." He told G-Baby as he was answering the call.

"Naaw, nigga, you the one with the jokes, pressing ignore and sending a nigga to voicemail." Don's voice came over the phone.

"What's up, big bro? I was talking to G-Baby. She got all kinds of jokes early this morning. What's up though?" C1ty had to restrain himself from laughing at the face G-Baby was making while she was putting jelly on her biscuit.

"I figured you was going to forget. Blood we're supposed to link up this morning and go over that shit I told you about yesterday." Dell knew his little brother would forget. Shit he couldn't blame him G-Baby's little Mexican ass could throw down in the kitchen. When it came to her cooking, his little brother would probably forget a breakfast meeting with the president.

"Aw damn, brah. I'm not even gonna lie; I did forget. Me and baby eating breakfast now."

"It's good, I'mma bout to get me some shit right now. Just make sure to hit me in a minute and we'll catch each other in traffic."

Chapter 11
A few hours ago

Zoey Poppins sat behind the tinted windows of a Chevy Impala listening to the sounds of "Free Yotta Part II." She was an avid fan of his music but "Free Yotta Part II" and "Young Boy" with Oakland native Iamsu were her favorite songs. The music was turned down low, as not to distract her from what she was doing. She also didn't want the music to draw any attention from someone walking by. The world was full of nosey mothafuckas in Zoey's mind. She didn't need nosey mothafuckas all up in her shit.

Under the darkness of night, the all-black Impala was virtually invisible. Zoey didn't know how long she had been parked in front of C1ty's and G-Baby's apartment. She knew it had been hours though. She'd parked where she was just after sundown. Patiently she waited as she watched G-Baby come home by herself. Zoe badly wanted to put some hot shit into the body of the little Mexican chick who in Zoe's mind thought that she was all that. Discipline won out over her desires. She was here for a job and wasn't about to let anything or anyone get in the way of her doing that job. Not even herself.

She watched the apartment and street all night. Her patience had paid off a little after four in the morning, when she seen C1ty pull up and park. No more than fifteen feet or so in front of her. The headlights of a vehicle following C1ty's car is what prevented Zoe from immediately getting it popping right then and there in front of the apartment.

When the second vehicle pulled over without anyone getting out, she was happy that she hadn't responded too prematurely when C1ty pulled up. If she had, Zoey would've found herself in a crossfire between C1ty and whom she was betting was his security. The presence of C1ty's little security detail tickled Zoey Poppins. She couldn't understand how so-called street niggaz and gangstas could have security. Zoey Poppins figured if you was a real gangsta or a nigga who was really in the field, then you were supposed to be the mothafuck'n security.

Nevertheless, whoever the security was they had just given her an idea. Instead of wounding C1ty like she initially planned to do. She would use whoever it was inside of the second vehicle to send her message. She waited until just after six in the morning to make her move.

The Impala was parked about nine cars up the street from where the second vehicle was parked. It was on the opposite side of the street. This allowed Zoe Poppins to slide over and climb out of the passenger's side door without being noticed.

The sun was already an hour into ascending in the sky, but it still was a very chilly San Francisco morning. Traffic was light on the street. People had either already gone to work or were still inside of their homes getting ready for work. She hunched down as low as she possibly could. Trying desperately to conceal herself as best she could behind the parked cars on the street.

Zoey Poppins had driven over to C1ty's apartment directly after leaving the hospital yesterday. She hadn't even taken the time to change into something different. She smiled at the irony of it all now as she strutted boldly down the opposite side of the street. She was headed in the direction C1ty's security detail was parked. She made sure to step extra hard, so the click clack of her high heels were sure to be heard well ahead of her. Even the freezing cold air and gentle chilly breeze were her co-conspirators. The cold air had her nipples nice and rigid. They were so hard that they were bursting through the material of her nurse uniform. With her purse swinging in her hands with the rhythm of the sway of her hips. Zoey Poppins had the outer appearance of a young nurse on her way to start the early morning shift.

She felt the stare of the eyes on her body before she even reached the car they were in. It was a four-door charcoal gray BMW with light tints on the windows. Someone on the outside looking into the car could see the silhouette of the bodies inside but couldn't see the occupants in detail. She could feel the eyes roaming all over her body. When the driver's side window started to roll down, Zoey smiled within. Outwardly, she acted like she hadn't noticed.

"God damn lil' Mama. You make a nigga wanna shoot himself just to have a reason to need a nurse." The nigga in the driver's seat called out through the open window.

Zoey Poppins stopped and looked at the nigga. She stood back on her heels so that her phat ass booty stuck out. "Shit you going to need more help than a little itty-bitty nurse if that's the best pick-up line you got." She told him.

"I'm good then, ma, 'cause that wasn't a pickup line. I just needed to get your attention, and it looks like I did that. What a nigga really trynna find out is what do I call something as drop dead gorgeous as you? And please don't say beautiful because your way beyond that." He bit down on his bottom lip attempting to entice her.

"Now you're starting to get a girls attention, sugar." Zoey smiled and took a couple of steps forward up on the car. When she bent forward to rest her arms on the car's door, huge breast almost burst thru the top of her uniform. "My name's Zoey like Joey but with a Z. But all of my friends call me Zoey Poppins."

The driver's eyes got big. He looked over at the passenger with a smile on his face and repeated her name to the passengers. When he turned back toward her, his eyes stayed glued to her big breast. After licking his lips, he asked her, "So why they call you Poppins, lil' mama?"

She brought her free hand up and traced her finger along her breast. Slowly sliding them down her cleavage, while she stared seductively into his eyes. "Because I get shit popping lil' Daddy." She let her juicy tongue trace her lips before adding "why else would they call me that?"

This got both of the niggaz in the car excited. The passenger started rubbing his hands together. All sorts of perverted ideas and images were parading in his mind. The driver either couldn't help himself or he just didn't want to. He reached down between his legs and grabbed his hardened dick.

"Well Miss Poppins, I'm AJ of the Gas Nation. This my nigga Eddie Bo. What a nigga gotta do to see just how you get it popping?"

"Well ...." She brought her finder up and slipped it seductively in her mouth. Before sucking and slowly sliding it back out. "Why don't you let me put your number in my phone. I'll hit you up sometime later and we'll see just what we can put together." She reached down and opened her purse. Sticking her hand inside as if she was retrieving her cell phone.

"Now that's just what the fuck a nigga talking 'bout. I know exactly what we can put together." He was already picturing sucking on them big, milky, white titties while she was bouncing that phat ass white booty up and down on his dick.

AJ thought that white women were God's special treat for mankind. He believed white women were the sexiest and prettiest women on earth. Every time he fucked a white woman it felt to him that God was personally telling him that he was proud of him.

As she dug into her purse. She allowed her peripheral vision to kick in. She used peripheral to scan the street and make sure no one had come outside. She didn't need any witnesses or anybody else fucking up her plans.

"Nigga, I told you! I can always spot'em. It's all in the way they walk. All freak bitches got the same kind of walk. A walk that demands your attention. Part power. Part sex appeal. Like it's telling you, I know you see all this I got over here. Look at how sexy it is. But I better not catch you staring at it!" AJ was back looking at Eddie Bo as he bragged about his ability to spot and recognize a freak bitch.

Eddie opened his mouth, getting ready to say something in response. Instead of words, the sound that escaped his lips was more like a pained groan. It happened at the same time AJ saw the side of Eddie Bo's face and head explode and spray the passenger side window with blood, brain matter and bone fragments. Simultaneously Eddie Bo's head violently jerked sideways like one of them zombies in that old Michael Jackson *Thriller* video. Immediately it jerked a second time.

The small popping sounds the bullets made as they flew out of the SIG 9mm with the silencer. Were like the sounds champagne bottles made when someone popped the corks open. This didn't register inside of AJ's mind. He couldn't believe what the fuck he just seen.

"Damn! I always thought that my walk was more of a nigga bring yo ass here, a suck on this phat juicy pussy!" The sound of her sweet voice got his attention.

He turned his head back to his left. Back to the beautiful white Goddess that resembled the model CoCo.

"That's the only downside about fucking with you white bitches. All y'all are crazy as fuck!"

"Koo-Koo! Mothafucka!" She squeezed the trigger with two rapid percussions.

Again, the small popping sounds were followed by the far side of his head exploding. The inside of his head spray painted the inside of the car. Right after AJ's lifeless body let out a long loud, wet fart. Evidence no doubt of the body losing it bowels at the moment of death.

Zoey Poppins slowly stood completely up. She took a moment to look around to make sure the street was still empty. She opened her purse and dropped the gun back inside. The foul smell of human shit hit her nose just as she turned and walked away.

As she walked away, she began singing. *Let's Get It Poppin* by Jim Jones featuring Jha Jha & Princess, altering the song lyrics to insert her name into it. *"We get it Poppin Zoey, Let's get it Poppin Zoey, We get it Poppin Zoey, Let's get it Poppin Zoey...."*

She stopped mid-stride. An idea came to her mind that was too sweet to ignore. She turned back to the car and spent a few minutes bringing her idea to life. She worked as fast as she could because whatever AJ had eaten smelled worse than death as it came out his ass.

The time as she strolled away from the car singing her tune. She did so while imagining the look on C1ty's face when he walked outside to find his security dead with the letters TIO written across the windshield in AJ's blood.

Back inside of the Impala, she pulled out her cell phone and made a call before driving off.

De'Kari

Chapter 12

A vacation sounded like a good idea to Rick. To say he needed and deserved one, would be the understatement of the year. He has been pushing full tilt or straight Beast Mode for going on two and a half years now. That doesn't include his earlier years on a steady and consistent grind. A hard grind that was improving his position and standings in the game. To put it plainly, Rick was a self-made factor. He carved out his own stake in the game and made sure that mothafuckas in the jungle they called San Francisco knew, understood, and respected his mothafuck'n position.

Along the way to the top, his tea has spilled enough blood in the streets to fill three Olympic size swimming pools. He himself was personally responsible for most of it. He received the handle Spank-G early on because he was quick to spank a niggaz ass for the smallest of reasons.

A little over two years ago an unfortunate event would break the hearts of thousands while altering the lives of hundreds. That was when the Feds took down what they called The Big Black Mafia. It was believed to be the largest crime syndicate in all of San Francisco's history. Second largest in Bay Area's history behind The Neva Die Dragon Gang. The Bay Area's Original Black Mafia.

When the Fed's took down Big Black, a large hole was left in San Francisco's underworld. It provided the perfect opportunity for Span G and his team. And they took advantage of it in a real way.

Now they were the top of the food chain. They were the head of the totem pole. Instead of relaxing and enjoying the good life. They were all grinding twice as hard as before. The fight to make it to the top wasn't shit compared to the fight to maintain their position at the top. It was nonstop Go.

He picked up his cell phone to call his wife and tell her that he canceled his meeting and was coming home. They were still newlyweds and although his new wife understood the rules of the game. She still wasn't happy with the amount of time he was giving her. She told him that she could put up with the fact that most of their marriage would consist of him having to be in the streets more than he would be home. She just wanted him to spend as much time as he possibly could with her for these first few months. He had to admit, her request was pretty reasonable. He just still couldn't honor it. Too much shit was going on.

He changed his mind about calling his wife. Deciding that it would be better just to surprise her. As he was putting the phone back down it began to ring. Spank-G answered on the second ring. It was his cousin Dee, a twisted Lieutenant on his team. They discussed the new time for the rescheduled meeting and a few other things. Spank-G let Dee know that he was heading home to spend some time with his wife Aliyah. Spank made it clear before getting off of the phone that he didn't want to be bothered.

Ten minutes after getting off of the phone, he was pulling up in front of his house. It was a little past midnight. All of the lights were already turned off. Thinking to himself that Aliyah must already be asleep. He was glad that he had not called because he would have awakened her.

He made his way in the dark to the kitchen. He reached into the refrigerator for a bottle of Dom Perignon and a carton of orange juice. Spank always kept a bottle of two of Dom in the refrigerator on chill. He poured two glasses, then made his way in the dark to his bedroom. The house was a nice old house. One of them ones built at the turn of the century during the big boom in California. It was a three bedroom, two bath upstairs and downstairs two-story house. He made his way up the stairs carrying a dinner tray with the two glasses of Mimosas that he'd already made, with the orange juice and opened a bottle of Dom P to put in it.

As he was climbing the stairs, Spank thought he heard something downstairs. He stopped. His instincts and street smarts kicked in instantly. Years of being in the field living that street life had honed and sharpened his senses. He used these heightened senses now as he closed his eyes and mentally scanned every inch of the first floor. He stood as silent as a statue for over a minute. Listening. Ready!

After another full minute went by without him picking up the slightest peep with his ears. He continued to make his way to his room. Aliyah always left the door to the bedroom open. She always said she felt caged in with the bedroom door closed. Like a prisoner locked away in solitary confinement.

He stood in the open doorway for a moment. Staring in the dark at the silhouette of the woman that gave meaning to his life. At the darkest hour, she was the one to offer his soul a source of light. The thought of what she meant to him warmed his heart as he stood there. He could tell that she was sprawled across the bed. This made him smile because Aliyah was a wild sleeper. She was always hitting him in her sleep.

Spank stepped into his room and turned on the light switch using his elbow. The tray slipped out of his hands. It fell on the floor. The champagne flutes filled with mimosas knocked against each other and shattered. The orange juice and champagne spilled all over the thick, expensive carpet.

For the first time in his entire life fear took hold of his body. Gripping his fragile heart. He was too scared to move. The fear had him frozen like a deer caught in the headlights. He managed to blink his eyes. Hoping with all of his soul that the image before him would disappear. Praying that somehow the bloody, mutilated corpse that was laying on the bed would somehow vanish and be replaced with a sleeping Aliyah.

He blinked his eyes again. His soul bled in the form of tears as he stared unbelievingly at the form of Aliyah's lifeless body. She laid completely naked with multiple gun shots to her naked breast. Though he only stood there motionless for a few seconds. It felt like hours that he was tormented with the site.

Movement snapped Spank-G out of his paralysis. It was as slight as a feathers whisper, but he saw it. Instantly he ran to the bed.

"Liyah, baby!" His tearful voice called out as he cradled her body. "Oh my God! Baby please! No...why?" The tears cascaded down his face as he stared down at her face.

"I-I-I... L-L. Love.. yo-you...R-R-Rick..." She said his name so low that he almost didn't hear it.

She died right there in his arms. There was no need for him to check to make sure. The piercing stabbing pain he felt in his heart told him that she was dead. He held her lifeless body tight. Rocking back and forth while he howled at the top of his lungs. The sound resembled a prehistoric beast that was roaring in a state of rage caused by tremendous pain.

Rick bolted straight up out of his sleep in a seated position. He was roaring at the top of his lungs. Sweat covered his entire body from head to toe. His bedding was soaked through with perspiration. Once the yelling left his head and actually reached his ears, he stopped. He had to blink his eyes a few times until his vision came into focus. Reality of where he was slowly began to dawn on him.

He turned his head to his left. Sitting there like she always did whenever his nightmares woke them both up. With a look of concern and worry written on her face was Trina. When he saw the look of worry on her face a tinge of guilt struck him. He looked from her worry filled face to her huge breast.

There was nothing sexual on his mind. The nightmares were so frequent that Rick had learned he could judge the level of intensity the nightmare had on him, by the effects it had on Trina. The easiest way to do that was to pay attention to her breathing. The rise and fall of her breast let him know that she wasn't as worried tonight as she had been on some other nights.

He took a deep breath. Wiping his face with his hand before saying, "sorry I woke you up Ma."

"Rick, every time you have one of your dreams, you say you're sorry and I'mma tell you the same thing I always tell you. And that is, you'll never have to feel sorry about being a real man." Trina leaned over and gave him a kiss on his cheek. "It's almost time to get up anyway. Why don't you take you a hot shower to wash all the bad memories away. While I change these sheets and start on breakfast."

Rick did just that. After Trina climbed out of the bed headed for the linen closet. He got up and walked to the shower. He knew how lucky he was to have found a woman like Trina. Once they began seeing each other more on a serious level. He opened up to her about his past. Revealing to her just how deep his feelings were Aliyah. What happened to her as well as how deep those feelings that he had for her still were.

Instead of feeling some kind of way as most woman want about him still having feelings for the woman, he was married to that was murdered over fifteen years ago. Or feeling like they were in competition with the memory of Aliyah, Trina thought it was the most tragic real love story that she had ever known. Trina never had anyone love her the way he had loved Aliyah. It was one of the reasons it didn't bother her that he still had feelings for Aliyah or the fact that he suffered from Post-Traumatic Stress Disorder behind losing her the way that he did. Trina was a remarkable woman and Rick knew this.

Most lesser women would have gotten fed up and left a long time ago. Trina was cut from an entirely different cloth than most women.

When he stepped out of the shower. He exited the bathroom with a towel in his hands drying off. The sheets had already been replaced and the bed made by the time he came walking back into the room. As he was drying off, his cell phone began ringing. He walked to the nightstand and picked it up. A smile came over his ace when he saw who it was that was calling. He knew the phone call could mean only one thing. Good news.

"Hello?" He answered. Masking his anticipation. "Good morning, Daddy." Zoey Poppins voice was filled with excitement. "It's been a long day and night for me. But before I headed in to get some much-needed sleep. I just wanted you to know that it indeed is going to be a very, very beautiful day."

"Is it now?" These were the words that he had wanted to hear.

"Yes, Daddy," she replied. "Very beautiful indeed."

"Indeed, we shall see." No other words were spoken.

Rick hung up the phone and got dressed. Trina wasn't quite finished with breakfast, so he went into his study. He spent the time getting some papers in order and getting ready for a speech he was giving later on. A little while later his niece walked in.

"Good morning, Uncle Rick." She saw him as she stood inside of the open doorway.

He looked up from his desk. "Good morning, Ebony. Come on in. How are you doing this morning, sweetheart?"

The resemblance she had with Rick's late wife; Aliyah, was unbelievable. Ebony was Aliyah's brother's child. Her brother was murdered in Lakeview another district in San Francisco when Ebony was just a little baby. Rick and Aliyah had taken Ebony and raised her as their own. When Rick was set up and went to prison, Ebony went to live with his mother. As she got older it was her love that kept him strong enough to keep fighting and believing things would work out on his appeal.

She walked into the study. "I'm doing good, Uncle. How about you?" she asked him as she sat down in the chair across from him. She could've been Aliyah's daughter instead of her niece.

"You know me honey. I'm good as gold and right as rain."

"Do you got anything for me?" She knew he was trying to conceal something. She figured that he must've had another one of his dreams.

"Later on I want you to get a hold of the Mexican. Then go and meet him. It's time for him to re-up. I need you to handle it because I have that engagement today."

"Okay, Uncle. I'm on it. That shouldn't take me anytime and I don't really have anything else to do."

"That'll be good. You can take Zoey with you if she's up. I want to let her sleep in, I just got off the phone with her and she sounded tired. She had a late night."

Trina came walking into the study. "Good morning, Ebony, honey. Y'all come on to the kitchen. Breakfast is hot and ready. We can finish discussing business at the table while we're eating."

"Good morning, Trina. Girl, you know anytime you get down in the kitchen you don't have to say nothing but a word and I'm there. Come on, Unc, my stomach is over here doing cartwheels now in anticipation of that good food." She stood up. "Don't worry about a thing, I'll take care of that as soon as we're done eating."

"Y'all go on ahead. I'll be right behind you." Rick had one more thing to take care of first.

"Rick, please don't make me have to come back in here and get you." Trina jokingly warned.

"I won't baby."

De'Kari

Chapter 13

When Chino got the call from Ebony telling him that she would be meeting him instead of El' Negro. He thought it only natural, they should meet at a hotel under the guise of two lovers meeting up for a rendezvous of love making. Naturally he never thought she would go along with the idea.

He was utterly shocked when she agreed. Not as shocked as he was when she came walking thru the door to the room. He couldn't call her beautiful, she surpassed beautiful a long mothafuck'n time ago. She was absolutely gorgeous. She had a face that inspired poetry and a body that tempted the gods. The outfit that she wore might as well have been body paint. It hugged her body enough that Chino's eyes could easily make out every single detail of the voluptuous body that was underneath.

When she first came into the room, he offered her a drink. She turned down the alcohol but accepted a cold bottle of water. Now she sat across the room from him on top of a bar stool. Her phat juicy lips wrapped around the top of the water bottle taking a sip while curiously watching him.

Chino could feel his dick coming to life. Hardening by the second as thoughts of what she could really be doing with those juicy lips played in his mind. He actually licked his lips and bit down on his bottom one as he mentally saw those lips encircle the head of his dick the way they were encircled around that water bottle.

Ebony brought the water bottle down from her lips and matched Chino's stare with one of her own. The intensity grew.

"You got something on your mind Chino?" She challenged him seductively.

Chino wasn't one to back down from a challenge. He looked her dead in her eyes from across the room. "I got a whole lot of shit on my mind. But you may not be able to handle my thoughts."

"Mmm, I see. Now them thoughts wouldn't happen to be erotic or sexual in nature, would they?" She was toying with him. They both knew that.

Chino watched her. Her middle finger circled slowly along the top of the bottle. Her legs were crossed left over the right. Giving him just a small glance at her thick upper thigh. It was just enough. His dick was pushing hard against his pants like a Rottweiler desperately trying to break free from its leash. Did she really want him to make a move? Was she willing to give him some ass? Or was she playing him the fool.

Fuck it! He decided to take his chances. "More like pure, unadulterated, animalistic lust."

"Wow would those thoughts be the reason you're sitting there looking like you wanna eat a bitch alive?" Ebony could clearly see the bulge of his dick print pressing against his pants.

"Daaamn right! Gobble yo' lil' ass up like dessert." Chino could feel his blood rushing through his body. He didn't know that his pupils were dilated, but they were.

The bold, confident way he spoke turned her on. Ebony could feel the walls of her pussy flooding. She was so wet. She wet her lips with her tongue. Slowly she uncrossed her legs. Chino's eyes became wide like saucers.

Satisfied that she had him completely stuck and trapped in her spell, Ebony raised her skirt up and opened her legs as far as she could out the way. Revealing the fattest, juiciest, prettiest pussy that Chino had ever seen. It was smoothly shaven with the exception of a small patch of hair above the clit in the shape of a small heart. The pussy lips glistened from the fluids that were leaking out of a pussy that was on fire.

"Then what are you waiting for?" She managed to open her legs a little more.

Chino was on his feet and across the room in a blink of an eye. He went down on his knees in front of Ebony's open legs. She scooted further. Only a small portion of her huge ass remained on the bar stool. He buried his face between her thighs and let his mouth go to work.

She tasted even better than he imagined. As his tongue attacked her clit, Ebony's scent drove him wild. He couldn't get enough.

Ebony couldn't believe how good the little Mexicans niggaz head game was, it was fire. His tongue expertly circled and teased her pulsating clit. He alternated from attacking the clitoris to plunging his tongue deep inside of her. Coating his tongue with as much of her juice as he could. Before she knew what he was doing, Chino reached around taking ahold of each of her ass cheeks in both of his hands. He buried his face as deep into her as it would go and started sucking on her clit like it was a pacifier.

Ebony couldn't take that shit. She grabbed the back of his head with both of her hands and fucked his mouth. It wasn't long before a powerful orgasm erupted deep within her, rocking her to the core. Her entire body spasmed out of control. The orgasm was so powerful she became lightheaded. For a minute Ebony thought she would actually black out.

After the orgasm passed, she was out of breath. Chino softly licked up all of her juices. He was ready to sink his dick as far into her as he could. With the pussy tasting as good as it did. Chino imagined it would feel like Heaven. He kissed her pussy lips once more before standing up. He started unbuckling his Fendi belt. A confused look came over his face when she pulled her skirt down and started fixing her clothes.

"What are you doing?" Chino didn't have time to be playing no fucking games. His dick felt like it was ready to explode.

"Umm…. What does it look like I'm doing? I'm fixing my clothes back." Ebony had a look on her face like Chino had just asked her the dumbest question in the world.

"I-I can see that, but why? We're just getting started that was just a little taste"

Ebony chuckled. "Exactly. That was just a taste, nothing more. You said you wanted to gobble me up like desert, so I let you. Let me thank you too cause a bitch needed to get a hit off something fierce. And shit what can I say your head game was bonkers. That was just what a bitch needed." She stood up off the bar stool and picked her clutch off of the bar. "But now I got shit to do. So, I can't stay and talk about it. Who knows, if you're lucky, I might just let you taste it again." She turned and walked to the door.

Chino was fuming. He couldn't believe this back bitch just played him like she did. He wanted to knock the Holy shit out of her ass to protect his manhood. Yet he could still smell her sweet intoxicating scent on him. His taste buds were alive with the flavor of her sweet nectar. Fuck yeah! He wanted to taste that shit again.

Even after she'd closed the door to the room, Chino stood there licking his lips. Savoring the flavor of the remnants of her juices on his lips. His aching dick still throbbed and jumped in his pants. If only he could have bent the black bitch over the bar and fucked her hard from behind while thinking about her big black ass smacking against his thighs. He unzipped his pants and pulled his dick out. He continued to think about his dick sliding inside her phat, juicy, pussy, while he jacked-off. He stroked his dick hard and fast. Matching the rhythm in which he fucked her in his mind.

His cell phone threatened to fuck up his visual when it started ringing inside of his pocket. Chino didn't stop stroking. He reached into his pocket and grabbed it. He only opened his eyes long enough to find the answer button after swiping his thumb up on the screen.

"Yeah, what's up?" he grunted. The news he received pissed him off. This caused him to grip his dick even harder and stroke it faster.

The more that was said on the phone the angrier he became. The harder he jerked off. In his mind Ebony was screaming at the top of her lugs while he drove his dick into her pussy as hard as he could. He felt his nutt starting to build.

"I-I'm.... on my way." Just as he managed to get the words out, he nutted.

A thick stream of semen sprayed out from the head of his dick. He let the semen spray all over the floor. In his mind he'd pulled his dick out of Ebony's tight, wet pussy, and shot his nutt all over her big, round, black ass.

When he was done, he grabbed the set of keys Ebony had left on the bar. They were to a Ford Taurus parked in a specific spot in the parking lot. The trunk was loaded with dope. He stepped over the stain his nutt was leaving on the carpet and headed out of the door. She was still on his mind.

***

Chino pulled up to the trap a little over an hour after driving the Taurus out of the hotel's parking lot. The moment he pulled into the driveway, soldado's came out of the house. A couple took up spots as lookouts. The rest tended to Chino and the pickup. They worked quickly and efficiently. Chino didn't bother overseeing them as they unloaded the drugs from the car to the house. He left that to Smokey. Instead, Chino went inside to look for his brother.

Trucho had a worried look on his face when Chino came in. The look only worsened when he saw his brother walk into the room. Trucho was on the phone getting an update from the home girl Angelina. He put his index finger up letting his brother know that he needed a minute. Chino walked over to the mini refrigerator they kept in the corner and grabbed a Heineken. He sat down on the old leather couch and drank his beer while Trucho talked on the phone.

When Trucho first called he told Chino in code what had happened. So, Chino knew they'd been hit. He just didn't know the details of what happened nor the full extent of the loss. Most mothafuckas would be focused on the loss itself. To Chino the full details of what happened were more important. Someone had disrespected him, and he was only interested in finding out who it was. He had something special for whoever it was.

Trucho hung the phone up and looked at Chino. Even though he hadn't done shit wrong fear reeked from his pores like funk.

"Almost two hours ago some fools ran up in the spot over on and took everything. They killed Stomper and Lil' Ace. That was Angel Eyes on the phone. She's over at San Francisco General. That's where the blacas (police) took Casper and Baby Thumper. I had her go down there to see what she could find out." Trucho's eyes roamed all over Chino. Desperately trying to get a read off him." She just called to give me an update just before you walked in. Doctors told her Baby Thumper took three bullets, but all three bullets hit nonverbal places. They say he's going to be fine." His looked saddened and his voice became solemn. "She said that the doctors don't think Casper's going to make it."

Chino took a deep breath attempting to still his nerves. He didn't give a fuck about nothing this fool just told him. As far as he was concerned all the homies knew what tie it was when they go put on the set. This was all part of the game. Some days were good, some days were bad. All a mothafucka could hope was that in the end, the good days out numbered the bad. And pray you were able to at least enjoy some of the shit you hustled for before it was all over.

He knew his brother wasn't clearly able to think the way he did, so Chino was patient with him. "What do we know about the mothafuckas who did this?"

Trucho could hear the strain in his brother's voice. It made him more nervous. "I-I had W-Weco and Smokey ask the neighbors some questions and the fools who were out in the area. All we got was a couple of cars filled with Mayates raided the house. No one knows who they were, but they say that it was about six to eight of them."

After the shooting in front of the store the other day, Chino wasn't surprised to hear that it was blacks that robbed them. He just didn't understand why any blacks would have a problem with his people. Afterall it wasn't like he didn't go to extremes to conceal all the fucked up and conniving shit that he'd been up to. A part of him told Chino that Lil' Dooka was behind the recent attacks. Lil' Dooka must have found out that Chino was moving in on his territory and taking his business. These were the thoughts inside of Chino's head.

"Tell the homies to be at the park tonight. I got some shit to figure out before I decide how we gonna deal with this. For now, I want you to make sure that the shipment is secured. That everybody gets what they're supposed to get and that our spots are all running the way that they are supposed to. Double the security at all of the spots. I want them mothafuckas guarded like Fort Knox. I'm sure word is going to get back to the big homies. By the time it reaches them I wanna make sure we took care of the mothafuckas who did this. And I wanna make sure they see that, that little shit ain't do nothing to us. Chino finished the rest of his beer and stood up.

"What about Baby Stomper? You want me to have a few of the homies post up at the hospital with him to make sure he's straight?"

"What?" Chino turned and looked at Trucho like he was crazy. "Fuck no! Fuck Baby Stomper. This shit is all a part of being in the game, being a Norteño. I want you to tell that bitch to stay with him until he's good enough to leave. Tell her to call you the moment the doctor tells her it's okay for him to come home. Then I want you to send Smokes and another solid homie up there to pick him up. Once they do have them take him somewhere and kill him. What good are any of them fools to us? They couldn't even protect themselves or their shit from some lousy as Mayates."

Trucho wouldn't dare comment. Not when his brother was already talking about killing some shit. Instead of saying anything critical, he simply said "Okay."

When Chino walked out, Trucho picked up his phone. He needed to make a call.

De'Kari

Chapter 14

"Man, fuck, man.... fuck!" Nardy yelled out in frustration to no one in particular.

Nardy was beyond frustrated. He was pissed, angry, hurt and yes.... he was afraid. Normally he would work toward masking his fears so none of his brothers would know that he was afraid. Today though he didn't give a fuck about trying to mask his feelings. Not for his brothers, not for no bitches, and not for the strangers. Nobody! Nardy couldn't give a fuck about what anybody thought of him. He let tears fall down his face while his heart fell out of his chest.

All around the room the sounds of people crying could be heard. Here and there a few women would or screamed out in a display of agony. Budda, Meri, Turk, Lil' Dooka and the rest of the thugs were in the back of the church. All strapped up and ready for whatever in case the sucka side tried something. Nostalgic feelings ran thru most of those bodies as memories of Bubz funeral played in their minds.

Budda wasn't out on the streets for Bubz' funeral. He had heard what happened. What the suckas had done to Bubz moms. It was some pretty fucked up shit. Yet Budda was a nigga that fully understood the rules of the game and he accepted how this shit went. Because of this he didn't shed a single tear. Instead, he sat quietly observing the room. Waiting patiently for MoMo's funeral to be over so he could begin his reign of torture.

Budda had never had any dealings or run-ins with C1ty or the 357 niggaz. In fact, Budda had never even heard of them niggaz. To him the band of brothers represented Double Rock. So, in Budda's mind all Double-Rock niggaz was going to pay. Young, old, in the streets or in the house it didn't matter to Budda. Any nigga he caught out of bounds that was from Double Rock was getting business. Rather a nigga was with the shit or not!

The doors to the church opened drawing everyone's attention. Miranda came storming into the church. She was a mess. Her hair hadn't been combed for days. Her eyes were swollen like she'd been crying for just as long. Wrinkled clothes covered a body that had recently last weight from lack of eating. She openly cried loud as she made her way to the front of the church where the casket was. Tears stained her face and snot ran from her nose.

Some people gasped at the sight of Miranda. Others pointed at her and whispered. They were the ones that weren't close enough to the circle to know that. Miranda was Momo's baby mama. They'd been together since junior high school. Along the way they watched as they each grew up and grew apart from each other. She chose law school while he chased the streets.

"Fuck MoMo! Why huh? Why couldn't you listen to me?" She'd finally make it to the casket. She was staring down at MoMo through tear-stained eyes. "I loved you with all of my heart Mo was that not enough? What about your daughter? She wasn't enough for you to choose us over the streets. Huh MoMo, was the streets and your friends more important than me and your daughter?" She really began crying now. Screaming and asking God why. He took her Baby Daddy from her. A couple of MoMo's female cousins walked over to Miranda trying to comfort her.

Initially, Miranda accepted the comfort. Hugging and crying in the embrace of one of the cousins. When they tried to guide her away from the casket to an empty seat. Things went south.

"No. no…no! Let me go!" Miranda broke free from the cousin's embrace and ran back to the casket. She grabbed the front of the suit jacket that was on the body and yanked on it. "MoMo, why God damnit? Why couldn't you choose us? Huh? Tell me!" She was becoming hysterical. "Why did you choose your fucking lil' friends? Fuck Tre-Four! Fuck TIO! Where are they at now Mo? Where the fuck are yo lil' bitch-ass friends? You loved them lil' wannabe bitch-ass niggaz more than us, but they didn't even love you enough to watch your back. How come them bitches ain't die with you? How come you're lying here instead of Lil' Dooka's bitch ass! Or that fagot ass nigga Nardy.. huh? Why…." She was yelling at the top of her lungs.

Fuck this shit! Nardy jumped up and rushed to her side. He draped his right arm around her shoulders. "Come on Miranda. We know your hurting sis, but you throwing us off with all of this. Come on. Let me help you."

"W-What?" She looked to see who was holding her. Once she seen who it was, she went berserk. "Get yo fucking hands off of me you black mothafuckas!" She shook and struggled getting out of Nardy's embrace.

"Man, I'm serious. You throwing me off Miranda. You better pipe down."

"Don't you tell me what the fuck to do! I'm not scared of you Nardy!" She hauled off and slapped the shit out of him.

People in the church were shocked. Their gasps was louder than her slap. Nardy didn't hesitate nor did he take the time to allow the sting of the slap to subside. He punched Miranda in her jaw like she was a grown ass man. Her jaw broke instantly. She was unconscious before she hit the ground.

"Stupid bitch!" He was standing over her unconscious body getting ready to stomp the shit out of her.

Lil' Dooka caught him just in time. A moment later Miranda's head would've been bouncing off of the floor. Nardy spun to his left to see who had grabbed him. The look on his face said he was ready to fuck a nigga up. He relaxed once he saw that it was his cousin.

"Nard, chill out nigga. Everybody's watching you!" He growled into Nardy's ear.

Nardy didn't calm down. He was fuming. The punk bitch had the nerve to call him a bitch! He wanted to stomp a mud hole in her pun ass. He didn't give a fuck about her being MoMo's baby Mama. He did check his composure.

4-Boy and Waka picked Miranda's unconscious body up and carried her to one of the empty rooms in the back of the church. The rest of the funeral wasn't off with no problems.

***

After MoMo's funeral all of the members of TIO were inside of Auntie Dee's apartment. They'd all decided that they would keep her apartment. Auntie Dee's had been their hang out since they were kids. While all of their parents were in the streets chasing money together, the kids would all hang out at Auntie Dee's playing their video games and telling stories of their dreams of one day growing up to walking in the footsteps of their parents.

So even though Auntie Dee was gone, they couldn't abandon her place. It would be like abandoning her, they all thought. As if now that she was dead it was time to move on or some fuck shit like that. By keeping the apartment, they were keeping her memory alive.

4-Boy, Waka and Mari were all seated on the couch. The same couch MoMo and TG were on the day they got shot. Reco, Turk and Nardy were all seated around the table in the dining room with Fayzo and Pop. Budda was in the back room on the phone taking care of something. He couldn't hear because Mari and Nardy was too loud. So, he went in the back.

"Mari man you throwing me off with that shit! Nigga I don't care if it was yo bitch! A mothafuckas put their hands on me, I'mma put my mothafuck'n hands on them. You throwing me off with all that, that was the homies bitch shit. Bitch should learn to keep her fucking hands to herself.

"Nardy you gotta be smoking dick nigga, if you think you'd put your hands on my bitch. Nigga ain't nobody touching my bitch but me. Any nigga otherwise fa'sho smoking dick." Mari didn't give a fuck about none of that shit Nardy was talking. Nardy was dumb ass out of pocket for putting his hands on MoMo's baby Mama like that.

"What Mari, you think you sick or something? Nigga yo bitch could get it and you could get it too! Nardy stood up. His hand was inches away from the handle of his .40. He didn't like Mari anyway so if the nigga gave a reason, Nardy was going to blow his fucking head off.

"What bitch!" Mari jumped up too.

Mari knew that he would beat the fuck out of Nardy's little boney ass. The little nigga was 6'0" and only weighed 160 lb. Mari would easily dog walk Nardy. What Mari didn't know was that Nardy didn't have any fucking intentions on doing no fighting. If

Mari thought he was sick he was going to air his mothafuck'n as out.

Mari stepped toward Nardy. Nardy's hand grabbed the butt of his .40.

"That's what you bitches been on?" Budda came walking into the room. He looked very pissed off. "We out here burying mothafuckas left and right. Y'all got the opps feeling like they sick. Instead of taking it to them bitches, you bitches in here bout to kill each other."

They both looked at Budda. The truth of his words stabbed at their conscious like daggers. They were too embarrassed to talk. They stood there instead with stupid looks on their faces.

Budda looked at the rest of the niggaz in the room. They all could see the fire in his eyes. Turk knew the look mor than anybody. He'd seen it too many times. Budda was ready to kill some shit. He pulled his attention back toward Mari and Nardy.

"If you mothafuckas gonna be on some bitch shit, be on that shit somewhere else. Nigga I'm only 'bout that Fo shit! If it ain't Tre-Fo shit its hoe shit. Instead of arguing like lil' bitches, I say we go pull some skitz and let them mothafuckas know what time it is."

"Now that's what the fuck I'm talking 'bout!" 4-Boy called out from the couch.

Fayzo was in the dining room next to Pop. Fayzo wanted to ride on them suckas just as bad as anything, but there was one problem.

"Shit ain't bout to be that simple Budda. Them bitch-ass niggaz done must've went into hiding somewhere 'cause it ain't no sign of them anywhere!" Fayzo waited to see how Budda responded to that.

"What! Nigga, fuck them 357 niggaz. If them bitches wanna hide let'em. As far as I'm concerned them niggaz from Double Rock. Since its up with them niggaz, its up with all of Double Rock! Everybody from O-Hunnid an opp. We done with Double Rock. Them niggaz can deal with each other." In Budda's eyes an opp was an opp. Didn't matter who it was. If you were an opp, then you were a target. And if you fucked with the sucka side then you could get it too!

"We 'bout to fuck them Double Rock niggaz up!" Reco was getting juiced as well, off of the rest of their energy.

"What about Dooka? Anybody gone tap in and let him know the play?" Waka just threw the question out there, but it was really directed to Budda.

"That nigga gone miss this 'cause he taking care of something else. It's all Greezy with Dooka, you niggaz just get ready. Bu, nigga, I don't think it's smart for you to be trynna pull skitz and you just bailed out?" 4-Boy wasn't trying to put Budda on the spot but God damn it's one thing to be gangsta. It's another being fucking stupid.

"Bitch, what the fuck you think I bailed out for? You think I bailed out to go to more funerals? Bitch, I bailed out so we wouldn't have to bury nobody else!" Thoughts of his precious daughter entered his mind. She was his world, but he had to push the thoughts out of his mind.

Budda was about to hit the killing fields, and wasn't no reason for love on the killing field.

Chapter 15

Sgt. Dudley made sure to have both eyes wide open and on alert as he drove through the Potrero Hill neighborhood. It was known to be one of San Francisco's deadlier neighborhoods. This was one of the reasons Sgt. Dudley had his eyes on high alert. The second was his reasons for being out this night in the first place.

Too many bodies were beginning to pile up in his area. Although the body count inside of his investigative area was always high. They were on course to setting a new record, and it was all behind the ongoing feud between TIO and 357. Sgt. Dudley was tired of all these fucking monkeys within this shit-stained zoo called San Francisco. When he first joined the academy, Dudley had high aspirations in helping clean up the city. That was before he realized just how fucked up San Francisco really was.

Year after year. Slowly but surely, he came across more and more vile scum. Then he stumbled across the corruption. The city was filled with so much corruption. It was hard to come across another hardworking, honest, good clean cop. It seemed none of the elected officials were clean. They were all guilty of one sort of offensive or another. From taking bribes to having dealings and ties with the criminal organizations that ran the city's underworld. Soon he gave up hope. He joined the rank and file of the corrupt.

He was thinking about his partner and her tight little ass when he spotted the man he was looking for. Dudley pulled in front of him and rolled the window down.

"Get in." He called out without even looking at the man.

"God Damn Dudley! Not right now man. I gotta make some money. Tanisha's birthday is in a couple of days and I gotta get her a gift. Dean hated when Dudley came to his block. It was just one of the small prices he paid for being a bitch nigga.

"If you don't get yo black ass in the car. I'll run you in for the crack I know you got on you. Plus, I'll plant this .38 on you that I know has at least one body on it. Then I'll come give Tanisha a birthday gift. I bet she could really move that big ole ass got."

Dean hated Dudley with a passion but what could he do? He has been Dudley's snitch for almost two years now. Ever since Dudley busted him with nine ounces of crack that he had just bought off of his patna, Manny. Dean agreed to set Manny up in exchange for himself not going to jail. That one decision saved Dean's freedom but cost him his soul in return.

"Man.... Fuck!" Dean opened the door and got inside of the vehicle.

Dudley didn't speak. He simply pulled off. They rode in silence as Dudley drove two blocks, turned the corner and parked.

"So, what did you find out for me?" he asked Dean as he turned the lights off.

"You were right. It's them little mothafuckas from Fo. They call themselves TIO. It stands for Tear It Off...."

He cut Dean off, "Mothafucka, I know all that shit. Yo black ass better tell me some shit I don't know!"

"I-I-I'm trying. I-It all started behind on of them TIO niggaz disrespecting this nigga C1ty's girl. C1ty and his team ain't friends, their family. All brothers and two cousins or some shit like that. Anyway, that nigga that was killed in his driveway. That was their little brother. The word on the street is they vowed to kill every one of them TIO niggaz. And now them 357 Mobb niggaz are up on the score board. First, they killed the little nigga that night of the concert. They shot up the funeral killing the little niggaz whose funeral it was moms and a couple of niggaz. They got Auntie Dee and lil' MoMo. It's like Lil' Dooka and them ain't got no answer for them niggaz."

Dudley cut Dean off again "Is Lil' Dooka the leader?"

"That's just it. He called shots like he was their leader. Shit he even moved like it. But in truth they ain't got no leader. If they did, it would be that nigga Bu."

"Who the fuck is Bu?" The name was foreign to him. Dudley knew everybody in Hunters Point yet he never heard of a nigga named Bu.

"Budda" Dean told him.

Now that was a name Dudley did not want to hear. Budda was a royal pain in his white ass.

Dean continued, "Word is, that nigga Budda home. He supposedly bailed out on a ticket. They say he's taking MoMo's and Auntie Dee's deaths hard. Said he don't give a fuck about 357, he holding all Double Rock responsible." Dean figured that little bit of info would light a fire in Harry Potter's fucking ass.

He sat there in the passenger seat with his hand in his jacket pocket holding onto the handle of his snub-nose 38. If Harry Potter got on some bullshit Dean wouldn't hesitate to pull the .38. Everybody in the hood knew about Sgt. Dudley antics. That's why they called him Harry Potter.

Dudley sat quietly. Mulling over what he had just heard. The last thing he needed was for Budda's little ass to be free on the streets, pissed off with a gun.

They both heard the sounds of a woman screaming coming from down the alley Dudley had parked in front of. It sounded like the woman was yelling in front of someone. Sgt. Dudley looked over to Dean.

"Get out!"

Dean didn't have to be told twice. He opened the door and did his best track star imitation.

Sgt. Dudley turned his headlights back on and put the car in drive. Then he turned into the mouth of the alley. A little more than halfway down the alley he spotted a couple arguing. The man was of average height and a little on the stockier side. He looked like he was ready to punch the woman until Dudley's lights lit up the alley. The woman was dark skinned about 5'8" wearing a white fishnet top with nothing underneath and a pair of boy shorts that left the entire bottom half of her ass jiggling as it hung out of the shorts. It didn't take a rocket scientist to see what was going on here.

Dudley got out of the car. The guy seemed scared when he saw Dudley's badge. The woman seemed annoyed.

"What seems to be the problem here?" Dudley asked both of them although he was sure he already knew.

"W-Well officer.....I-I......" The guy began.

"This mothafucka here won't give me my mothafuck'n purse. That's the mothafuck'n problem!" She spoke with confidence that said she wasn't lying.

Dudley looked at the guy's hands. He was holding a knock-off Louis Vuitton purse.

"Sir. Give me the ladies purse." He held out his hand.

"I-I.... S-She-She stole my wallet. I want my wallet back!" He sounded like a little fat kid who was saying they wanted ice cream and cake and not just ice cream.

"Give me the purse." Dudley's voice was stern this time.

The guy handed it over. His hand was shaking. Dudley started to open the purse when the guy told him that he already checked the purse. The woman stood there looking at him. Her eyes challenging him. From this angle he had a clear view of the front of her body. Her titties were about the size of softballs. She had bid dark nipples that were just as visible as the rest of her breast. Dudley's dick jumped in his pants.

"Mam could you turn around please?" His eyes were anticipating the sight they were about to take in.

She spun around slowly. She made her ass cheeks jump when her back was completely turned toward Dudley. He wondered just how good it would feel to ram his cock as deep as it would go into her. By the time she'd turned back around she had a smile on her face.

"Well, you can just about see every inch of body and I don't see no wallet...." The guy started to say something, but Dudley cut him off. "Goddammit! Don't you try to cut me off! Now I say she ain't got your damn wallet. You need to walk out of this alley right now and take your ass home before I take you to jail for soliciting prostitution." His eyes dared the motherfucker to say something else.

Reluctantly, the guy did as he was told. When he'd turned out of the alley the woman turned to Dudley and thanked him.

"Favor for a favor sweetheart." He hungrily licked his lips and grabbed his cock.

She didn't need any instructions. She walked over to him and undid his pants. When she had his little dick out, she thought it wasn't hard because it was so small. She got down on her knees and began sucking it. Dudley was loving it. He loved black bitches. He thought a black woman was the sexiest fucking thing on earth. He looked down at her as she sucked him. She wore her hair in a curly blonde mohawk. The sides were still black, the hair was silky and wavy.

It didn't take long before he felt like he would blow his wad. He pulled back, taking his dick out of her mouth. When he told her that he wanted to fuck she laughed.

"Unh-unh, honey. You gots to pay if you trying to get between these sugar walls."

Dudley felt disrespected. "Bitch I'm not giving your stinking ass not one red cent. Fuck you think you are? Now bend your black ass over the hood of my car!" he yanked her to her feet.

"Hmm mothafucka if you want that tiny, little, pink dick of yours to go inside of me you...." She couldn't finish the sentence.

Her making fun of his little dick infuriated Dudley. He punched her in her big ass mouth with an over-hand right.

"You think your cute bitch!" He punched her in her stomach and caused her to double over. She cried out in pain. "Think you're a fucking comedian!" He drug her over to his car.

He was panting like an animal. The sight of her big jiggly black ass caused his blood pressure to rise. He forced her to bend over the hood of the car. He bent down on top of her until his mouth was next to her ear. I'm going to teach you some Goddamn respect, you worthless black bitch!"

She couldn't respond, the blow to her stomach had snatched all of the wind out of her. Dudley punched her on her left side for good measure cracking two of her ribs in the process. The pain caused her to piss herself.

He snatched her shorts down until they were by her knees. Her black ass was phat and juicy. He couldn't help himself. He licked all over her round chocolate ass cheeks. Even sticking his tongue as far as it would go in her asshole.

Then he stood up and grabbed his little cock. He rammed all three and a half inches as hard as he could inside of her ass hole.

Then he fucked her as hard as he could. He loved the sight of his pink dick as it disappeared into her black ass. Her ass cheeks made a clapping sound as they bounced off of the top of his thighs.

"Ain't no worthless.... unh.... black bitch gonna ever.... unh.... talk to me like you c-crazy bitch!...uhgh." When she didn't respond, he punched her in the side again. This time breaking ribs. She screamed out in agony and pain. This caused him to reach his peak. He came deep into her asshole. He pumped erratically until all the semen was out of him.

He pulled his cock out of her sore and bleeding asshole. He shoved his dick back into his pants without bothering to wipe it off. He snatched her off of his car. She crumbled and fell. In too much pain to do anything other than lay in the fetal position right there on the cold filthy concrete. Dudley climbed back in his car and drove away. He never glanced in the rearview at the bruised and battered woman that he left nearly naked, hurt and in need of medical attention.

If he had of looked, he would've seen the guy that he had run out of the alley, as he came creeping back in like the little varmint he was. Had Dudley have had just an inkling of decency to look in the mirror at the woman he'd left. He would have seen the varmint add to the woman's pain by repeatedly raping her right there in the cold dark alley. When he finished sexually assaulting her the varmint would kill her then scurry away into the darkness like the rodent that he was.

Chapter 16

Ebony finally reached the park. She pulled over and parked her car about seventy-five feet from the front of the park. It was the closest she could get due to all of the vehicles that were already there for today's event. The event was supposed to attract a lot of important people, rich people. Ebony could clearly see the media vans and the police that were security for today's event.

Ebony hated being around these uppity rich mothafuckas. She hated being around corrupt, self-righteous, two-faced politicians even more. If she had things her way, she'd kill them all. Today wasn't about them, she had to remind herself. Today was all about her uncle and what he was trying to accomplish. Her uncle donated $250,000 for the remodeling of the park. They offered to rename it after him. He told the committee of parks and environment that he didn't donate the money for any sort of recognition. Instead, he told them that his sole purpose and motivation was to give the kids a nice safe place that they would want to come play at. He believed the kids needed to have more things readily accessible to them then they currently had.

Ebony got out of her car and made her way to the park. She'd called Zoey like her uncle wanted her to do, before coming to the event. Zoey told her that she had something more important to tend to. So, Ebony came alone. As she made her way closer, she wondered how her uncle would take that Ebony liked Zoey. She was tenacious. Although she could be a loose cannon at times, Zoey was a very valuable asset.

She went through the hassle of two checkpoints. Security was tighter due to the mayor being at the event. She could hear her uncle. He was in the middle of his speech. She got even closer so she could hear him.

".... You see far too often people cry about the poverty, or the violence and even the drug crises that's going on in our inner cities, our projects, and our ghettos! Far too often people are oh so eager, oh so quick to point out the many things that are wrong with the hood. But when it's time to do something about it, when it's time to come out of them fat pockets and kick in so that something could be done about them problems. Then some people get quiet. They develop amnesia and selective memory.

"Now I'm not here to judge them people, look down on them people or put them on front street. I got some advice for them. Since you get quiet when it's time to get to solving the problem why don't you just shut up altogether, about the problem...." People in the crowd gasped and murmured. "That's right. I'm not a politician so I can get away with telling you. If you're not going to be part of the solution, shut up! Because you are a part of the problem It's okay though because we got this! We will be a part of the solution ourselves. It's okay if everyone else forgets about us.... It's alright. Simply because we won't forget about ourselves when everyone gives up on us and our future. It's all good! 'Cause we're not giving up on ourselves! We got this!"

I didn't donate the money for the park for any kind of recognition. I simply gave back to the streets of San Francisco because I am from the streets of San Francisco. Like our mayor, I grew up in the streets of these same hoods that I am now focused on rebuilding. The first step in making the streets safe for the kids to provide safe places for the kids to go. Once we secure them a safe haven to go to. Then we can tend to the business of removing the poisons that are polluting our streets. We can cut out the cancers that are killing our streets......"

Ebony's phone vibrated in her pocket. She pulled her attention away from Rick's speech to check her phone. Initially, she didn't recognize the number that sent her a text message. A smile spread across her face; realization settled on her mind once she read the text message. It was from Chino:

3:31 p.m.
I hope you don't think that you played a mothafuckas with that little move you pulled. I didn't sweat you cause ain't no thirsty niggaz over this way. Girl I been a Boss. If you don't know you better recognize. Listen, I'm not one to play games. I like your style and I Luv your flavor. I've never tasted candy that sweet. Why don't we get together and see what's good?

Straight Beast Mode 2

P.S.
I'm still hungry!
I J S.

Her pussy slightly tingled at the memory of how good his tongue felt buried deep into her pussy. While his lips danced around and sucked on her pussy lips, she could definitely see herself letting the super confident Mexican get another mouthful. But she would make him sit and sweat for a minute. Just to show him that she was the one in control, not him.

The event ended a little while later. Of course, her uncle had to shake hands with and trade a few words with people, before they could make their way home. Ebony followed Rick in her own car. His driver was a trusted longtime friend named O'Jay. Though O'Jay always acted the part of loyal driver, he was also Rick's bodyguard. O'Jay was a killer from way back but still loved to get his hands dirty. Rick had all sorts of enemies when he first came home. Mothafuckas who didn't want to see him free as well as the dick sucking, shit eating, low-life muthafuckas that betrayed him. O'Jay knew his homeboy would need him and he came, guns blazing.

Back at the house, the three of them sat in the den discussing business. Rick valued O'Jay's opinion, plus the killer's loyalty had been tried and proven over and over. So, Rick welcomed him to the table. O'Jay knew enough that if Rick needed to lean on and rely on him, it was no problem. However, Rick vowed no one would ever again be able to betray him. So, O'Jay didn't know too much.

"She didn't tell you what this other business she was working on was?" Rick wasn't really worried about Zoey Poppins. She was a free spirit when he first met her. It was one of the things Rick liked about her.

"Naaw, she just told me that she had something more important to take care of. Whatever it was, she said it would help the cause." Ebony told him as she checked her I.G.

O'Jay was eating a huge turkey and cheese sandwich that was twice as big as anything someone could buy out of any sandwich shop. He took a big bite before asking Rick, "You want me to tap in and see what's good?"

"Tap in? What the fuck does tap in mean?" Rick looked at O'Jay like he was a space alien.

"It means to check in. All the kids now-a-days say tap in instead of check in." O'Jay took another bite of his sandwich. To him it was fucking common sense.

"Nigga I'm forty-four years old. I don't give a fuck how the kids are talking these days! Little muthafuckas can't figure out how to tie their own fucking shoes. Fuck I need to sound like them for?"

"You gotta stay with the times Spank or they'll fuck around and pass you by." Pieces of turkey and cheese flew out of O'Jay's mouth as he said Rick's old street name.

"Fuck it. Let'em pass me by." Rick shook his head at the site of the food landing on his friend's shirt.

The way O'Jay ate disgusted Rick. He didn't say anything about it because it would only cause O'Jay to talk and spit more food out of his fucking mouth.

"So, what about the broad? What you want me to do?"

"Don't do nothing. Zoey's always been a free spirit. An independent thinker if you will. Ever since I've known her, she's moved to the sound of her own drum. She'll be alright. And if she says she's doing something for the team, then you better believe she's doing exactly that." Rick picked up one of the pre-rolled blunts on his desk and lit it.

He always kept anywhere from ten to twenty blunts rolled and sitting inside a dish on his desk. It was Ebony actually who saw to it that the dish was never empty. The funny thing is Rick has never seen Ebony roll one blunt or put one inside of the dish. But he damn sure appreciated the fact that she did it.

"Whatever you say." O'Jay couldn't care less. Rather he tracked the little white bitch down or not didn't matter to him.

"Did everything go alright earlier?" Rick asked Ebony after blowing out a big cloud of that good shit.

Ebony knew he was referring to the meeting between her and Chino. Briefly her mind went over his tongue game again. The thought made her pussy tingle again.

123

"Yeah, everything was smooth," she answered. Then she thought if his head game had her pussy jumping this long afterward, she definitely was going to let him do his thang again. Who knows, if he's good enough and she's feeling herself, she might just see what the dick do.

"That's good. I think I'm about ready to double his workload." Rick expressed.

"You think he's ready for that?" Ebony didn't look up from her phone screen.

"He ain't got no choice but to be ready. He said he wanted to sit at the table with the big boys. Then he's got to be ready to make big moves. In fact, I'm going to let him know that you dropping him off something else in two days. Everything is going smoothly and according to plan. Doesn't mean we can't have an ace in the hole in case we need to speed things up some or even alter them a bit. That move with them Mexicans from out of PA might've actually helped us out a little bit. Now we got the Low involved as well. A little ahead of time but they're involved, nevertheless. They think them Mission Street fools were behind the shooting. Everything set for an all-out war." Rick knew exactly what he was doing. He set a goal, figured a plan and was now executing that plan with precision. He was reminding muthafuckas who Spank-G was." Oh, I almost forgot C1ty called me earlier. He said he wanted you to know that everything was on schedule." She logged out of her I.G. and put her phone in her pocket. She stood up. "If there's nothing else, Uncle, I'll see you in the morning. There's something I need to take care of."

"Alright, baby. I'll see you in the morning." Her exit was perfect.

Ebony's birthday was coming up. Her leaving would allow Rick the opportunity to discuss some ideas of doing something special for her with O'Jay.

De'Kari

Chapter 17

"...That right there is what the fuck I be talking about! P you're throwing me off brah. Why would I lie to you? Huh, tell me that. Why in the fuck would I lie to you?" Lil' Dooka was on the phone with his little brother, P-Smacks.

"But I'm saying tho', Dook. The shit you talking, don't make sense. What the fuck do some Migos from E.P.A. got beef with us for?" P-Smacks was only eighteen, but he wasn't no fucking dummy.

P-Smacks was Lil' Dooka's younger brother. At one time they were thick as thieves. That's back when all Lil' Dooka knew was that Low shit. The two brothers were actually from the Low. The problem was all of Lil' Dooka's niggaz were from the Fo. To Lil' Dooka it was bigger than just choosing a side. It wasn't about the Low and the Fo. It was about his niggaz. His family. He didn't give a fuck who had a problem with it. So, Lil' Dooka stopped claiming the Low and started representing TIO. In P-Smacks's eyes and everybody else's from the Low, Lil' Dooka was reppin' TIO not the Fo.

Lil' Dooka didn't too much feel like putting up with the third degree from P-Smacks. Little brother or not a mothafucka wasn't going to question him like they were the police. Still, he wasn't trying to get in no beef with his little brother over nothing, so he took the time to run it all down to P-Smacks. Finishing up with the news he had gotten from Shark Montana.

Shark Montana had hit Lil' Dooka not too long ago and informed him that some Norteños from his city was spreading the word that they lit up Sunnydale. Once word got to Shark, he tapped in with Lil' Dooka thinking it was him and his folks that got rolled on. Lil' Dooka told Shark that them niggaz sprayed up the Low not the Fo. Shark let him know that he was there if Lil' Dooka needed him regardless.

P-Smacks had his phone on speaker. Kino heard everything that Lil' Dooka just said. It all made sense to him. At least it made more sense then, them bitch-ass cowards from Mission trying to get at them. Lil' Dooka told P-Smacks to tap in with Shark so he could put him up on game.

After giving P-Smacks a line on Shark, Lil' Dooka got off the phone. He gave that shit as much time and energy as he was willing to give. He had to focus on the shit that he was doing. He hated the fuck out of South San Francisco. Everything about the city got on his fucking nerves. Starting with the name itself, South San Francisco. It made it seem like it was part of San Francisco, but it wasn't. It was its own city. Nowhere near connected to his city. South San Francisco was overrun with Mexican gangs and wannabe gangstas. As far as Lil' Dooka was concerned there wasn't nothing but bitch-ass niggaz in South City.

He started hearing a loud rattling sound coming from the rear of the vehicle. To Lil' Dooka it sounded like the noise was coming from the trunk. He couldn't have that. The last thing he needed was a San Mateo County Sheriff Deputy or a South City cop to pull him over.

At the next corner, he decided to pull over and check to see what was causing the noise. He thought about leaving his Glock in the car, but niggaz didn't do that in Cali. Even in a bitch-ass city like South City, shit could still get active. That's how Cali was. Especially, inside the Yay Area. He stepped out of his Infinity with his Glock on his hip. He looked around, checking his surroundings. A cold chill ran down his spine. He ignored the strange feeling that came over him and jumped back in his ride. He reached into his pocket for his cell phone, which had just begun ringing.

The loud piercing sound of tires screeching against the pavement got his attention. A moment before he turned his head toward the sound, the thunderous boom of gunshots rang out. The first bullet ripped through his left shoulder, spinning him around. His finger was just pressing except when a second bullet pierced his bicep causing him to drop the phone.

Lil' Dooka reached for his Glock as more and more bullets invaded his body. Whoever was shooting at him was not playing; they were hell bent on killing him. He returned fire, letting off a few shots blindly as he ducked behind the passenger side of the Infinity.

Straight Beast Mode 2

His body was in excruciating pain, but he couldn't focus on that, he had to gather his strength and find a way out of the situation.

The shots were coming from a pick-up truck that was a few feet behind his vehicle. Lil' Dooka only got a glimpse of the shooter as he was running to duck behind the car. He could've sworn it was the white bitch. The nurse from the hospital with the blue and red hair. A burst of bullets ate up the back of the Infinity. Hard plastic from the taillights and glass from the window flew through the air with the bullets that ricocheted.

When the shooting stopped, Lil' Dooka raised up and sent his own bullets at the driver's side of the truck. Had his adrenaline not been rushing through his body so much, he would have realized no one was behind the truck. Zoey Poppins had used the last spray of bullets as cover to give her enough time to run from behind her open driver's door to the front of Lil' Dooka's Infinity.

Dooka reloaded his gun and started shooting at the truck again. The sound of someone kicking a soda can startled him and saved his life. Without thinking he threw himself over the trunk of the Infinity. This move would put him in the middle of both shooters, he thought. But the eminent threat was behind him.

Zoey squeezed the trigger of the MP5 again. The bullets sliced through the air like razor blades slicing cocaine white. Yet, they were a few inches off target, missing Lil' Dooka. He rolled over after diving over the trunk and came up firing. He was tired of playing Black Ops with this white bitch.

Unfortunately, she wasn't playing games with his ass at all. This time when he rose up, her bullets chewed his ass up like a swarm of angry killer bees. His body moved like Neo in the Matrix, but he didn't dodge this shit. Lil' Dooka couldn't believe it. After all the skits he done pulled, he got caught slipping himself, by a bitch!

A white bitch at that!

He stumbled backward until he finally tripped over his own feet and fell. He was in a tremendous amount of pain. Why wasn't he dead? He didn't know, but he damn sure wasn't about to do any complaining. He frantically searched for his gun. It fell out of his hand while the bullets were hitting his body. His vision was blurred be tears he didn't realize were there. It made the job of finding his gun that much harder. His hand knocked against cold metal.

"Naaw lil' Daddy." Zoey kicked the gun out of his reach just as his fingers were trying to wrap around the handle. "You ain't got no need for that no more. Shame on you trynna shoot a bitch," she teased.

"Bitch, what you think I'm supposed to sit here and beg for my life and cry like a bitch? I'm Dook, bitch I….." He couldn't finish because a fit of coughing seized his body.

"Naaw I was gonna be a nice bitch and put you of your pain." She looked over his bullet riddled body with a look of satisfaction, pleased with her handy work. "But since you wanna talk that Greezy shit I'mma leave yo bitch ass lying there until you bleed out bitch!" She drew her foot back and kicked him as hard as she could.

He was already in a weakened state, the blow to his head nearly knocking him unconscious. He did his best to get it together as Zoey walked away rapping the words to her favorite song. He was hoping the devil bitch was gone by the time he struggled to his weak feet.

When he made it to his feet he just stood there for a moment. Swaying left and right as he gathered what he could of his bearings. Then he stumbled and shuffled his way back to the driver's seat. Lil' Dooka didn't quite know if he could make it to the hospital, but he desperately had to get the fuck away from where he was. He thanked God no bullet had hit anything vital in the car as he sped away.

Lil' Dooka tried his best. He did everything he could to stay conscious. The last thing he remembered was seeing the name California Street on the sign as he turned right onto the street. He blacked out roughly thirty feet after turning the corner.

Nathalie Quintanilla-Guzman was laying on her bed at her parents' house. Like most nineteen-year old's, Natty as she was called spent most of her time all her different social media accounts. A great deal of that time was spent surfing the profiles of various models. Admiring their bodies and the lifestyles they were able to live because of their modeling careers. All the while secretly wondering if that could be her. But a great deal of time was spent looking for him.

Natty was 5'6" and weighed 134 lb. She had 32C-25-38 body frame. Long, shiny, brown hair to match her brown eyes, on a face Jennifer Lopez would die for. She couldn't see it herself, but little Natty was a real Mexicana bombshell. If she knew how many niggaz beat their dicks while looking at her Instagram pictures, she would probably begin to realize just how beautiful she was. Shit, Jennifer Lopez spent thousands on her body, and it still wasn't fucking with Natty's.

She was on I.G. watching the video of the shooting at Tanforan Mall. No one knows who uploaded it to Lil' Dooka's page because he was locked up when the video surfaced. But that bitch went viral faster than a mothafucka. Natty must've watched the video a thousand times. Lil' Dooka was so gangsta she thought to herself. For one nigga to get in a shootout with fifteen niggaz by himself, in broad daylight, in the middle of a mall. How gangsta is that shit! She found that attractive. She knew she was out of pocket because of what happened, but she couldn't help it.

Suddenly she heard gunshots, but she ignored them at first. It was normal hearing gunshots in the Bay Area. Almost anywhere you grew up in the Bay Area, you heard gunshots. But when the gunshots continued and she heard more than one gun, she grabbed her laptop and went into the front room. The sound of the shots told her that the shootout was pretty close. Natty knew that bullets traveled, and stray bullets killed more bitches than niggaz did. She sat on the couch and went right back to I.G. She stopped the video and started going through his I.G. page, Lil' Dooka was a fine chocolate mothafucka.

She was looking at his San Mateo County booking photo that was on his page when she heard the loud scream of tires screeching. Probably one of the shooters trying to get away from the other, or away from the scene. Seconds later she heard the loud sound of a car crash into something. It sounded so loud she jumped out of her seat thinking somebody crashed into the front of the house.

Natty ran to the front window to look outside. Sure enough, someone had crashed into the big Oak Tree that was in front of the house. She ran outside with no thought to herself or her safety. Her only thought was what if the person needed help. Her heart was racing with adrenaline as she approached the driver's door of the car. She tripped over a tree root that was pulled out of the ground, and nearly fell.

The car itself was completely totaled. She could see smoke and steam rising from the hood. As she got closer to the car, she could hear the hissing noise the steam made. When she got to the driver's door, she couldn't believe her eyes. Blood was all over the place. Not just some blood, but a whole lot of blood. The persons clothes were soaked with blood. Natty imagined he must have gotten shot multiple times. She reached into her pocket for her cell phone. She dialed 911 and was waiting while the phone was ringing. Suddenly he moved, and when he did, Natty gasped.

"911 what's your emergency?" The dispatcher's voice came over the line.

Natty took another look. A closer look. She wasn't losing her mind. When he moved his face became visible. She was looking at Lil' Dooka.

"911, Caller, what's your emergency?" The dispatcher repeated.

Natty hung up the phone and shoved it back into her pocket.

Chapter 18

Sgt. Dudley couldn't figure it out. Deon had never given him any bad information before. So, Sgt. Dudley didn't have any reason to doubt what he had told him. Yet he couldn't find anything on this C1ty kid. With the help of some of his contacts, Dudley was able to obtain the kids government name, yet De'Mario Albert' was as clean as the board of health. The kid didn't have as much as a traffic ticket. If he was really the young master mind that Deon insisted that he was, then maybe Dudley could possibly understand how the kid could manage to stay off the radar. Dudley just couldn't buy it.

His computer buzzed letting him know that the search he conducted on AVIS was completed. He brought his attention to the screen, simultaneously clicking the mouse to bring the screen to life. He read the results twice. The case was getting stranger and stranger.

His phone line started ringing. He ignored it for the first three rings finally picking it up on the fourth.

"Yeah, this is Dudley speaking." His eyes were still on the computer monitor.

"Sgt. Dudley, this is investigator Sgt. Jerome Baker from over at the Richmond Station." The voice was too smooth for a cop. Sounded to Dudley like he should've been some fancy type of singer'

"Okay Sgt. Baker. What can I do for you?" Dudley's attention was still on the computer screen.

His AVIS search had landed a match. Only it wasn't a match to a known suspect or any known fingerprint on record for that matter. It was a match to a fingerprint from another case that was uploaded into the system for a search.

"Well, Sargent, I'm the lead investigator of violent crimes over here at the 318. I've run into a lot of things over my years on the force, but I've never come into something like this." He paused for dramatic effect like detectives often did. "I'm investigating a string of violent armed bank robberies. Well, we managed to get a latent print off one of the robberies. Now this is where it gets interesting.

I ran the print through AVIS and got a match. Instead of a known suspect, the match was to a print off ' homicide that you're working on.

This got Dudley's attention. For the first time he took his eyes off the computer screen.

"Yeah, I happen to be looking at that this very moment. You say you're working on a string of bank robberies?"

"That's right. There's been six of them all together with the latest one occurring just yesterday. I believe they were all hit by the same crew. This is highly sophisticated, professional crew. My guess is, we're talking five or six members, possibly seven. They're in and out. Never going over three minutes inside. Getaway car always on hand. Switch car usually a half a mile away waiting. They tend to stray away from violence but believe me they will and have used violence when necessary or for effects...."

Dudley interrupted him. "What do you mean for effects?"

"Well not too long ago the same crew knocked off three banks all on the same street. All within a few blocks of each other. Just before this happened some son-of-a-bitch walked up and opened fire on a squad car with an assault rifle over on Haight and Ashbury. I think the crew did it as a decoy to draw the city's resources. I mean let's admit it, an officer down is going to draw law enforcement from all over which is what they had in mind when they decided to rob all three banks. Killing a police officer in broad daylight, that in itself, is pretty brazen. So is robbing three banks on the same street one after the next. In fact, I don't see no other way anyone could've gotten it done." Secretly Sgt. Baker respected the crew. Even somewhat admiring them for their level of sophistication and brazenness.

"What you just described doesn't sound like any of the guys that I have on my radar. I mean I'm dealing with a gang war possibly between three gangs. We're talking street gangs from the ghetto. They don't have the sophistication to pull off what you're talking about, nor do they possess the level of intelligence needed to pull off any of these robberies of the heart to kill an officer in broad daylight for that matter. Sgt. Baker, I don't know how the two prints are linked, but I assure you that your suspects aren't a bunch of gang bangers. Hell, maybe one of these kids has an account at one of your banks. That's more believable than the bullshit you're shoveling." Dudley's annoyance was clearly apparent.

"Sgt. Dudley, I understand how unbelievable this sounds. But if you would just consider...."

Sgt. Dudley cut him off. "Ain't nothing to consider Sergeant. You're wasting your time and have wasted all of mine that I will allow you to." Dudley had heard all that he was willing to hear. He hung the phone up in Baker's face. He couldn't believe the fucking idiot wasted his time with that bullshit.

"Who's wasting your time?" Morgan came walking up to the desk. Her arms full of files that she dropped on her desk.

Their desk were aligned so that they faced one another. It was easier to work on cases and brainstorm that way. It also made it easier to toss ideas back and forth.

"Some fucking dimwit from the 318 Station with some cockamamie notion that some of our ignorant, drug dealing, gang bangers have somehow acquired the intelligence and sophistication to become professional organized bank robbers."

"And what was he basing his idiotic hunches on?" Morgan

was more practical than her partner. She understood very well that although most criminals fit the mold for the types of crimes they commit. Oftentimes, one will find that sometimes nothing fits at all, and nothing makes any sense. But that doesn't mean that it isn't right.

"You know the prints that were lifted from the scene of the murder of Auntie Dee?" When she nodded her head yes, he continued. "Well, I ran all of the prints in AVIS and got a hit. Not off an actual known suspect, the hit was a match to a fingerprint search of the exact same print. It was lifted from one of the bank jobs that schmuck is working on."

"And you doubt that?" She threw out the bait.

"I don't doubt that he has the print. I mean, shit, he uploaded it into the system. The fact that it's in the database proves that he has the print. So, I'm not arguing that. I'm just saying it could have gotten there a million different ways." *Come on, nibble at that juicy bait*, Morgan thought. "Shit one of the guys could have an account, could've been there with a girlfriend or something. Hell, he could've walked in to get change and touched a counter or something."

"So, did you ask the guy what the print was taken off of?" There you go, bite that bait. She again thought to herself.

The stupid loo' that came over his face told Morgan that Dudley hadn't asked the question. The truth was, they didn't know much about the so-called 357 Mobb.

"I didn't bother wasting my time. If the dip shit had something of substance, he would've said so." He reached over and picked up one of the files. His way of saying that was the end of the conversation.

"Never know what he would've said if you wouldn't have hung up the phone."

Dudley ignored her last statement. As far as he was concerned, if she was that concerned, she could call the guy back herself. Since she didn't get the hint when he picked up the file that the conversation was over, he changed the subject. "Have you seen Gillispie?"

Gillispie was one of the lead detectives in the Homicide Division. She transferred over from the Sherriff's office a few years ago and has been kicking ass every sense. She had a cute face, nice ass, and a personality out of a fairy tale story. But she solved murders like she was Sherlock Holmes himself.

"She's right over your shoulder."

He turned his head. Sure enough, she was walking his way. The way she was moving, Dudley guessed she was on her way out on a call. He called out to her when she got close.

"Can't talk right now, Dudley," she answered in response.

"One minute," he answered back.

Gillispie paused right at his desk. "You got thirty seconds, sweetheart. I can't give you any more than that."

"When you get a free moment, I would like to go over what you have so far on the murderer you got on that kid that was killed in his driveway a couple of months back. I have reason to believe it's connected with my Sunnydale murders."

"Okay, I'll find you or give you a call as soon as I'm done with everything surrounding this latest case." She turned to walk away.

"What's the new one? Why is it so pressing?" he asked as he stole a glance at her large, round ass.

"Dead prostitute was found raped, beaten, and murdered in an alley over in Potrero Hill sometime last night. No one important. Your average prostitute. Young, pretty, dead. Only, we have on eyewitness on this. So, I'm rushing over there before those guys somehow mess things up and I lose my witness. I'll call you once I wrap it all up." She turned and walked quickly away.

The sight of her round ass swallowing the fabric of her parts as each cheek bounced up and down, on any normal occasion, would've driven him crazy. He couldn't savor the moment this time though. A prostitute found raped and murdered, the sound of that sent chills down his spine.

Morgan caught it. Sgt. Dudley was a male chauvinistic pig, who hounded women like the wolf in those Warner Brothers cartoons. She'd watched disgustedly over and over as Sgt. Dudley openly ogled the ass of every female that had even walked past his desk. Especially Gillispie. Every time she walked past his desk, Dudley stared hard at her ass and licked his lips like her ass cheeks were actual Christmas hams. Today he didn't even glance at her ass. Something about the dead prostitute had him shook.

De'Kari

Chapter 19

Fat Boy laughed after he hung up the phone on Chino. To him Chino sounded like a real puta, a real bitch, the way he was on the phone talking about niggaz shooting up his hood an' running up in a couple of his trap spots. In Fat Boy's mind instead of calling his phone crying like a little bitch, like he was doing. He needed to be getting back at them mothafuckas with some real fire! Being soft the way he was Fat Boy didn't think Chino deserved to be in a position of leadership. He didn't have the nuts to lead. Nevertheless, fuck him! None of that shit was Fat Boy's problem. As long as Chino had his shit for him everything was all good. If he didn't, then there would be a problem.

 Fat Boy was on his way to deal with Scarface. Just because the two of them had been friends since elementary, didn't mean that Scarface wasn't going to answer for getting jacked for the drugs in the first place. Fat Boy drove over to the spot that they had on Palo Verde in MidTown. It was a section of East Palo Alto that was known for its Back Streets. Instead of paved streets and sidewalks, most of the streets that made up the Back Streets were dirt roads and mounds. It was a perfect place for the violence that was carried on daily.

 The first thing he noticed when he walked inside of the house were the three homegirls who shouldn't have been there. June had one bitch sitting on his lap while he and Smokey played something on the PS4. All the bitch had on was a pair of shorts that were so small they looked like they would fall off at any moment. There were two other bitches sitting at the table in the dining room eating some kind of fast food or take out. They were all laughing at the story Hector was in the middle of telling

 The guys instantly got quiet the moment he walked in. The bitches who were ignorant to the fact that they weren't supposed to be there, kept right along laughing. In fact, the bitch that was sitting on June's lap hadn't even noticed Fat Boy had walked into the house.

"You niggaz is tripping. Turn that shit off and get these bitches out of here. Where the fuck that nigga face at?" Fat Boy was pissed, but his high-pitched voice was as calm as it would be if he didn't have a care in the world

Hector didn't hesitate to snitch his boss out. "He in the back room with Lisa."

The girls didn't appreciate Fat Boy calling them bitches, but they knew who he was. None of them wanted to risk getting on his bad side.

Fat Boy walked to the back room where Scarface was. When he opened the door, Lisa was riding Scarface reverse cowgirl. Her big ass titties looked like air balloons as they bounced up and down in rhythm with her riding his dick. Instead of screaming, her head was tilted back, eyes were closed, and she was talking that dirty slick shit in a low voice.

"Lisa get yo fucking clothes on, and you are your girls get the fuck out to here."

Instead of getting up off of Scarface's dick. Lisa grabbed one of her large breasts and put it in her mouth. She began sucking on it and riding Scarface even harder, while staring at Fat Boy with a mischievous look in here her eyes.

He had to admit to himself that she was a bad mothafucka. Under normal circumstances he probably would've walked up and stuck his dick in her mouth. Shit they would've turned this bitch into a group thang. Not today it wasn't that kind of party.

"If I have to repeat myself, then yo ass ain't going to be able to walk outta here at all." The look she saw on this face told her to get the fuck on.

Scarface knew he fucked up. He knew Fat Boy was pissed. The one thing Fat Boy always told him was never have bitches at any of the spots. Bitches couldn't be trusted, therefore they were a liability. And the only way to ensure a bitch wasn't their liability was to never have them at the spots. He also knew Fat Boy would talk shit to him for a little while, but he would forgive him. He always did. That was Scarface's problem, he never took anything serious. Thought he

Straight Beast Mode 2

would get everything handed to him on the strength of his older brother.

He thought wrong.

Fat Boy saw Lisa's body when she climbed off of Scarface. That shit was banging hard. He turned around and walked back to the front room. The other bitches were already gone. Lisa wasn't far behind him. She struggled to pull her yoga pants over her wide hips. She managed and made her way out the front, mumbling some shit in Spanish.

"What's up with y'all niggaz? Y'all sitting up in this bitch like it ain't no money to be made. Like y'all ain't got shit y'all supposed to be up in here doing. And you niggaz know the rules 'bout bitches being up in the spots. Who do fuck told y'all it was cool to be bringing bitches up in here?" He knew the answer; he just wanted to see who would stand tall and who would fold.

"I-I tried t-to tell him that the shit was against the rules, Fat Boy, but Scarface said that we take our orders from him and to let him deal with you." Right on cue, Hector gave it up.

"That's what he told you, huh?"

"Yeah, that's what I told them. Fat Boy, what you tripping for, homie? Our count is on point. Everything up in here is straight. So, I told the homies they could relax a little with some bitches. So what? Why you tripping?" Scarface was scared as shit, but he didn't want to lose face in front of his boys. Besides, ever since they were in the sandbox at Belle Haven Elementary, Fat Boy looked out for him.

"Oh, so you get this shit, right?"

"Yeah, nigga. I got this." Scarface felt a little relaxed since Fat Boy wasn't reprimanding him.

"Like you had that shit down the freeway last week, when yo' ass called me crying and sniveling, 'cause you let some niggaz take my shit!"

June had never seen Fat Boy lose his composure. This was the first time he ever heard him raise his voice.

"T-that was different. Them fucking Mayates caught us off guard Fat Boy." Scarface hated Black people because his brother was killed by a nigga.

"Nigga, if some niggaz would've run up in here, you would've been slipping again! They would've taken my shit again! Scarface, I've tried to put up with your bullshit 'cause I know you're going through some shit." He pulled out a chrome .45 from the back of his waistband. "But I can't have you running around doing whatever the fuck you wanna do. Not following the rules and shit. That shit don't look right. Then you can't even keep our shit safe. You make us look weak, Face. And I'm not weak."

The sight of the gun in Fat Boy's hand terrified Scarface. He began shaking violently as he cried and begged for his life. The display of cowardice didn't move Fat Boy at all. It only showed him just how weak Scarface really was. A mothafucka that weak didn't deserve to call themselves MMN.

June and Smokey looked on in disgust. All the tough ass gangsta shit Scarface was always talking. Now he was right here in front of them crying and pleading like a little bitch. They couldn't believe it. The only person in the room not judgmental to Scarface was Hector. He understood. In fact, he felt sorry for Scarface. Hector would never want to be in Scarface's shoes. Hector couldn't even begin to imagine how he would feel.

The sound of the big .45 was deafening. At a distance of about three and a half feet apart from each other. The force from the three slugs slamming into his chest knocked Scarface completely off of his feet. His body flew a couple of feet backward, crashing up against the wall. He was dead before his body slid to the ground.

Fat Boy turned to look at Hector. "If you told on him so easily, I know you'll tell on me if the po-po ever come asking questions."

Hector saw that crying and pleading didn't just work for Scarface and the two of them had been friends since they were kids. So, he decided to take another route. He bolted for the front door. The move was so smooth and sudden, he should've been a track star. He might have been elite.

He'd cross the living room in under three seconds. However, there was a love seat in between him and the door. Instead of trying to get around it, Hector decided to hurdle that bitch. He leaped like one of them African Gazelles. The slugs that left the .45 were faster. They caught his ass mid-air. The first bullet shattered his shoulder blade. The second blew his heart out of his chest. The third barely grazed his head. It didn't matter because he was dead anyway.

Neither June nor Smokey so much as flinched. They were real MMN soldiers accustomed to violence and the harsh realities of life.

"June, take over all of Scarface's houses and responsibilities. Hit me after y'all get this shit cleaned up and this spot back running, and we'll go over everything that I expect from you. Remember, my niggaz, there's consequences for this shit." Fat Boy tucked his gun back in his waist.

On his way out the door he looked at Smokey. Wondering if he could trust the seventeen-year-old or kill him too, Smokey didn't cower under his gaze nor break eye contact with Fat Boy. He decided, yeah, Smokey was solid and left.

De'Kari

Chapter 20

"I don't give a fuck about that nigga! Fuck Budda! That nigga don't mean shit. This still 357 Mobb! That nigga bleeds just as easily as any other nigga. We can't control what that nigga do. If that nigga declared war on the whole O-Hunnid Block tell niggaz to suit up. But that shit ain't on us. We gonna stick to the plan. That last job was a little off. Now we can't let this bullshit interfere with what we set out to do." C1ty was addressing his crew and family. "Now the OG done kept his side of shit for us. We've gotta pull through on our end. We're almost at goal. Let's not lose track behind this beef. Let's get this money and get out."

"Brah, you talking this petty beef shit like that's really what the fuck it is. Them bitch-ass niggaz killed our little' brother. Ain't nothing petty about this shit. This is a generational war and t's gonna be until all of them and theirs, ain't no more. You got shit backward little brah. That money shit is secondary this war shit is primary! Straight up." Don wanted the money like the rest of them. But after losing Wes all he thought about was killing them Sunnydale niggaz.

"Shit I feel you on that shit. I mean I got mad respect for the OG, but that nigga gonna have to understand, avenging my little brother is an obligation above all. And if he don't understand, this cannon will fa'sho straighten out his comprehension." Dell cocked his chrome .44 for emphasis.

This was exactly what C1ty didn't want to happen. Truth is he was surprised that he had been able to keep this conversation from happening for as long as he did. He knew his brothers were a hundred percent right. After Wes was killed, they should've torn the streets apart until all them TIO niggaz were dead. Here he was, a grown ass man going back and forth with some little ass kids.

He wanted to body them bitch-ass niggaz too. All he was trying to do was make sure that they had a way and a means out of this fucking shit when all was said and done, and the dust settled. He wanted to make sure they could get as far away from San Francisco and never have to worry about looking back. That was the bigger picture, and that's what he was focused on.

C1ty looked from his brothers to his three cousins. There wasn't any need for them to tell him what they thought. That shit was written on their faces.

"Alright, so y'all wanna turn the heat up on them little bitches?" he asked all of them.

"We got to, C1ty. They dropped three niggaz in the hood last night, and two the night before." CJ knew C1ty didn't want to hear the next part but shit it had to be said. "It's like that nigga Budda coming home has a mothafucka putting batteries in them niggaz backs."

"C1ty just keeping this shit G. We can really go to work and lay this murda game down on these little niggaz and fuck around and have the business end of shit back on track in a couple of weeks. I mean, after all, cousin, this that shit that a nigga really do. You feel?" The smile on Murda's face spoke volumes.

C1ty had been keeping them at bay really. Now it was time to take the chains off. It was time to teach them little mothafuckas what this shit really was.

XO leaned forward in his chair. "Shit might not even take that long. Especially once me and Murda start hunting."

What could he say? It was family over everything, and their family had been touched.

"Say less then. We are gonna shut everything else down and bring it to these mothafuckas." C1ty knew in his heart that he was making the right decision. Even though his mind told him he'd just fucked up.

"Aye yo, before I forget, I did some digging into what actually happened to them Gas Nation niggaz that were rolling on security that night." XO almost forgot about this shit.

"Ok, what's up?" C1ty looked over at him.

"Word is it was some white bitch that got them niggaz."

"A white bitch?" C1ty couldn't have heard him right.

"Yeah, some white bitch with blue and red hair. Apparently, lil' mana was walking down the street when one of the niggaz pulled her over and tried to holla at her. They talked for a minute and lil' mama drew down and fed them niggaz some hot shit. C-Note's cameras picked up the whole thing."

"A white bitch?" C1ty repeated.

"Blood, she was a bad lil' bitch too." XO threw out there.

"Whatever happened to the bitch you told me about that was in Wes's phone?" Hearing that a bitch was involved reminded C1ty about the call he and Don had the other day.

"Shit didn't pan out. I went to her house, her people's spot, and a nigga couldn't find her. It's like the bitch disappeared." Don paused briefly from rolling his blunt to look at his brother.

"Run through it again. She might have something good to tell a nigga. As for that white bitch, now that's a different story. That shit don't make no sense. Which is why we really got to pay attention to it. I'mma shoot to the house and send Genesis on a trip for a couple weeks. With her out of the area, I'll be able to focus more. I'll meet up with y'all later on tonight and we can get it in. Murda, since this is your expertise, you call the play."

That's all Murda had been wanting for. He nodded his head and smiled. It was game time.

***

Fat Boy didn't lose a wink of sleep from killing Scarface. If he was completely honest with himself, he knew he should have killed Scarface a long time ago. Fat Boy's loyalty to his childhood friend is why he hadn't done it a long time ago. But enough just was enough.

After killing Scarface, Fat Boy swung by Juanita's place and picked her up. He'd been so busy in the streets of that lately he hadn't been giving her no attention really. So today he was making it all about her.

"Babe can we swing by Three Brothers before we head out. I haven't had time to get any food and I'm starving," Juanita asked the moment she got inside of the Mercedes.

"Girl, you know you don't ever have to ask. I got you." He could go for a burrito and a couple of tacos. "You wanna go to the restaurant or the truck?"

"It doesn't matter, babe, you decide."

"Alright, I got you."

Since Juanita lived in Menlo Park, he was going to have to head toward East Palo Alto no matter what, both the restaurant and the food truck were in East Palo Alto. While he drove, Juanita kept bugging him. Trying to get him to tell her where he was taking her. That shit wasn't working though. Ten minutes later, they were pulling up behind the taco truck.

"What you want me to get?" He put the car in park and turned the ignition off.

She looked at him like he was retarded. "Boy, you know I always order the same thing, so stop playing with me."

"You never know. Sometimes people switch things up and try something new." He was hinting about the conversation that he had overheard her telling her sister about the other day.

"Not me, boo boo. I find something I like and I stick with it. I'm a loyal bitch." She knew damn well what the innuendo was 'bout. She'd seen his shadow in the open doorway when she was talking to Jessica She didn't trip because she didn't have anything to hide.

He let that linger and got out the car.

Fat Boy was looking up at the window giving the young Hispanic woman his order. She was all smiles and bashful eyes. He knew he was foul especially with Juanita sitting in the car no more than twenty feet away. He didn't give a fuck. He had to get at this bitch.

He was too distracted with the Piasa bitch to see the black Tahoe that just turned the corner. Juanita saw it though. A chill raced down her spine. She reached down between her legs for her purse that was sitting on the floor of the car. She never took her eyes off of the truck. Juanita was born and raised on the 1200 block of Hollyburne. She was a true hood bitch, and she knew every nigga from the hood. Those niggaz that were eye fucking them wasn't from the hood. She watched the truck as it passed and drove down the street.

Straight Beast Mode 2

She was still watching when it flipped a bitch halfway down the street.

She'd be damned if she was about to play with these niggaz. Juanita unzipped her purse and pulled out her Glock. The truck stopped in the middle of the street between the taco truck and the Benz. Three niggaz jumped out with guns in their hands.

Fat Boy was clueless. He was slipping. He was more concerned with how sweet and wet that little Piasa pussy was going to be. Then he was his own security, He loved Piasa bitches, Fat Boy believed them Mexican Nationals had the best pussy. It was super wet, and they fucked the way they danced that Salsa shit

Young Stubby was the first to come from behind the taco truck. Kino was only a split second behind him. Both of their arms were raised at the same time. Death was only a few feet away from Fat Boy.

"Fat Boy!" Juanita screamed.

The sound of Juanita's scream made Fat Boy the spin around instantly. It was too late! Young Stubby's and Kino's guns both barked simultaneously. Multiple slugs ripped through the flesh of Fat Boy's body. His body jerked and twitched like he was listening to that old school Keak Da Sneak song "Hyphy."

Juanita's heart dropped. Fat Boy w's the love of her life. She wasn't stupid She knew he fucked other bitches, but she didn't care because she was his queen. She finger-fucked the trigger. She sent wild shots flying over Kino's and Young Stubby's heads. However, only one of the slugs caught Young Stubby.

The sound of the bitch's scream got Baby Shoota's attention as well. He spun around in the direction of the scream. He didn't know how none of them had seen the punk bitch. It was too late for that now. She'd already got a warning off to the fat ass Mexican. The gun in her hand got off only a split second before Baby Shoota hit that bitch with some shit from the FN he was holding.

Juanita felt like a swarm of angry killer bees were stinging her body with fiery stingers all at the same time. But her focus wasn't on the pain her body was feeling. Instead, it was on the pain in her heart as she watched her man get gunned down. The pain of a broken heart gave her the strength to keep shooting. With twelve bullets already in her body a grim smile of satisfaction spread across her face as she watched the bullets slam into Stubby's back. No doubt, he was about to drop.

Juanita never got the chance to see Young Stubby fall and crash on the sidewalk, because Baby Shooter raised the FN slightly while he was shooting and sent a barrage of bullets into her head. Making that bitch explode like a piñata.

Fat Boy was lying on the ground twitching in a pool of his own blood. He knew he was going to die. He took too many bullets. His body was way too cold. Death was inevitable and he knew it. The life he lived death was bound to come one day. The only thing that he regrets, was not having enough time to at least take one of them niggas with him.

A line from a DMX song played in his head. *"Thought you was a killer nigga said you was a killer/swore you'd never run / nigga died wit' his gun still up in the holster/it's coming in the air, yeah it's getting closer."*

That was his last thought as the image of Kino walking up and standing over his head came into his vision.

"Nigga, fuck MMN, bitch!" Kino emptied the clip into Fat Boy's face.

Afterward, Kino and Baby Shooter struggled to get Young Stubby back into the Tahoe. Kino jumped in the driver seat and the three killers sped off, knowing that only two of them were going to make it.

Chapter 21

Word about what happened to Fat Boy spread quickly among the Norteños. There were even talks about going to war over this the problem was no one could say for certain who was behind the hit. There was plenty of speculation but nothing certain. Some of the homies even brought up the mysterious disappearance of the big homie Crazy.

Chino paid about as much attention to that shit as he did to a nigga on the streets beating his bitch. It wasn't his bitch. This was the same mind frame that he had regarding all the talk and rumors. Fuck Fat Boy If the nigger was really as hard as he acted and as gangsta as he thought he was. Then he wouldn't have got caught slipping.

Crazy on the other hand, Chino never expected him to bitch up the way he did. Chino was prepared to go to war with the O.G. Getting rid of Monster was the first step or the first strike in his attack. But Crazy bitching up made things easier for him. He wasn't going to lose any sleep over it.

Word on the street was somebody got to the nigga Dooka and knocked his fat ass down. Chino couldn't ask for shit to be going any better than what they were. Now he needed to move a few things around on the chess board and get ready for a swift checkmate.

He picked up his phone and called Trucho. "I want you and Snokes to take a couple of homies and go holla at them Tre-4 niggaz," he told Trucho when he answered the phone.

"Alright, homie. You got that." Trucho was eager to please his little brother.

Chino didn't think Trucho could pull off anything big without being coached. But all Chino needed them to do was create a little havoc, turn the heat up.

Soon he would burn them mothafuckas down!

He turned into the parking lot of the Hotel with a confident look on his face. Pride swelled his chest. He was about to fuck the brains out of this black bitch and show her he was "That Mothafucka!" By this time next week, he'd have a strong hold on Sunnydale. Then Potrero Hill, Visitation Valley and so on and so on until he was at the top of the food chain supplying all of San Francisco.

He got out of the car filled with swagger and made his way to the room, where Ebony was waiting.

***

This was the first time Chino let him call the play himself. Usually, Chino called the plays and Trucho would always be there putting in work like a good soldier. It was time for him to show Chino that he was ready to be a leader. After all they were brothers. It was only right that they ran things together, La Familia was forever!

He pressed and on the phone for the third time. He was trying to get a hold of Casper. He wanted to take Casper and Smokey with him tonight to carry out the play. He'd already gotten ahold of Smokey, who was going to meet Trucho at his house in an hour. Trucho decided to go to Casper's house since he wasn't answering.

Trucho got pissed off when he pulled in front of Casper's house and saw his Monte Carlo parked in the driveway. He figured the fool probably had one of the homegirls up in there and was getting his fuck on. Trucho was all for getting some pussy. He was pissed off that Casper ignored the phone. Anybody calling your number three times back-to-back should tell a mothafucka that whatever they were calling for must have been some important shit.

He banged on the door and waited for Casper to answer. When nothing happened, he banged again. This time calling out Casper's name too. Trucho wasn't about to fuck up his only chance because Casper was laid up with some bitch getting his dick wet. He reached for the door handle but paused when he thought he heard a noise.

He finally said, "Fuck it!" and opened the door.

Women never believed that Casper lived alone. His spot was always immaculate. Trucho never saw Casper's shit dirty. He had these little plants all over the place and a 200-gallon fish tank along the east side wall in the living room. The tank was full of all kinds of exotic looking fish.

Straight Beast Mode 2

"Hey homie Casper! Come on fool, we got some business to take care of!" Trucho called out as he slowly crossed the living room.

An eerie feeling came over him. He knew it was foolish, but he felt like somebody was watching him. "Say, fool you better not be playing games homie. I'm serious, Casp, I'mma fuck you up, homie." Trucho started to make his way down the hall. He was listening hard, trying to see if he could hear the sounds of someone fucking.

He didn't hear anything. Something was wrong.

He pulled his Glock off his hip. Casper could've been back there sleep, but Trucho didn't think so. And he didn't hear any fucking sounds, no screams, no moans, no squeaky bed springs. None of that shit. He knew what door Casper's room was, so he walked right up to it. Ignoring the other two doors.

His heart was racing in his chest.

His grip tightened on the Glock. He opened the bedroom door; Casper was in bed with a bitch alright. The way they were laid told Trucho they were dead. As did the bullet holes that riddled the bitches back. She had been riding Casper apparently when somebody came in shooting. The bitch had at least nine or ten shots in her. Trucho could only see an arm and part of the chest of whoever was under her. The tattoos on the arm told him it was Casper.

It didn't stink, so they hadn't been dead for long. This made Trucho walk over and move the bitch. He had to check to make sure Casper wasn't still alive laying there waiting for help. One look told him that Casper was dead as fuck.

He took a step back and shook his head, "Damn, homie, who da fuck did this to you?"

"I did."

Trucho turned around at the sound of the feminine voice. When he saw the white girl with blue and red hair pointing a 9mm at him, he realized he messed up by not checking the door to the other room or the bathroom.

"W-who the fuck are you?" Trucho asked.

He was confused. He'd never seen the white bitch a day in his life. *Is she one of Casper bitches?* he wondered.

He would never receive a verbal answer. The only thing he heard was the sound of the 9 mm as Zoey Poppins squeezed the trigger. Bullets flew into his stomach and chest. Trucho screamed out and dropped his own gun as he fell into the closet. Knocking the double doors off of the hinges and crashing into the closet with Trucho. Zoey walked up and sent three more bullets into Trucho's face. Making sure he was dead.

On her way out of the house, she was thinking that this shit was getting too easy. The fat Mexican bitch that was riding Casper was doing so much screaming they wouldn't have heard if a semi had crashed into the front of the house. There was no way in hell they would've heard her. Even if the fat Mexican bitch wasn't screaming her lungs out. Casper was moaning loud as fuck like a little bitch. When she opened the door, Zoey stood there for a minute and watched. The fat bitch had a huge juicy phat ass and she was working that mothafucka like a pro. Zoey even gets a glimpse of Casper's dick as the bitch rode up and down, grinding a popping.

Watching the two of them was doing something to her. Before she knew it, her small hands were in her pants rubbing her phat pussy. It Was soaking wet. The bitch on the bed screamed out she was getting ready to cum. She started riding his dick harder. Her big ass cheeks jiggling as she bounced harder. Zoey sped up her own rhythm. The scene was hot, but she knew what would make her cum. She shoved three fingers deep into her pussy and raised her other arm and started shooting.

When the big bitch arched her back because of the slugs tearing into her. Zoey immediately came all over her fingers. She continued shootin'. A couple of the bullets went through the bitch, but they didn't do much damage. Casper's down fall was the fact that he couldn't lift the bitch off of him once when she fell forward. He struggled to get free as Zoey calmly walked up and put the barrel of her gun right on the back of the bitch's head. The three bullets she fired into her skull made sure both of them was dead.

Standing there looking at her handy work, she played with herself again. She imagined herself on top of Casper riding him. And just when she was ready to climax, she would pull her gun and shoot him in the face. That image caused her to explode. The orgasm was so strong she got dizzy. After she gathered her composure, she walked to the living room preparing to leave. That's when Trucho pulled up and parked in front of the house. She had hoped he would leave. When she realized he wouldn't, she hid inside the shower and pulled the curtain and waited.

This time no one was outside. No one came and no one got in her way as she left the house and disappeared. At least she thought nobody had seen her. That's because she never saw him seated in the driver's seat of the money-green Buick LeSabre with the tinted windows. He waited a few moments after she left before he drove off.

De'Kari

Chapter 22

"My nigga, what you mean?" Budda was pissed. "Ain't nobody heard from that nigga and ain't none of you mothafuckas said nothing." He slammed his gun down on the table and stood up. "Did you mothafuckas forget that we in the middle of a fucking war? Or are y'all just that fucking stupid?"

Nardy was the first to speak up. "Man, you throwing me off with that y'all stupid shit, Bu. We didn't think nothing of it because you said you had him taking care of some shit when we rolled out on them Double Rock niggaz."

"Bitch! That was almost three days ago. You gotta be stupid if you think I'mma have the nigga doing something that's gonna take three days, knowing that we beef'n with niggaz. It's no wonder them bitch-ass niggaz been given y'all problems. You niggaz too stupid to go to war with niggaz. We got niggaz dropping left and right, but y'all not tripping that we ain't heard from brah in three fucking days."

Tuck, Reco, and Waka just sat there. They all knew how bad Budda's temper was. None of them wanted him to point his anger and frustrations in their direction.

"Budda, man. Come on, Budda, you throwing me off Nigga, ain't nobody stupid. Mothafuckas might have fucked up, nigga, but that don't make us stupid." Nardy was actually in Special Ed classes in school. He didn't like anybody calling him stupid.

"Bitch, I don't give a fuck what you saying, you are s-stu... stupid, bitch!" Budda stuttered to add emphasis.

Budda was the coldest killer out of all of them. That didn't mean a mothafuck'n thing to Nardy. He wasn't nobody's bitch, and he wasn't going to let nobody treat him like a bitch. Even though he was scared he bounced up from his seat.

"Bitch! I ain't stupid. You got one more mothafuck'n time to call me stupid bitch and we gonna have a mothafuck'n problem." Nardy was steaming.

Everybody could see it written on his face. They all knew how sensitive Nardy was about being called dumb or stupid. Budda didn't care though, and they knew that too. He was a master with that talking Greezy shit. Budda literally had no filter and didn't give a fuck. To make shit worse, he lived like he had a death wish.

"Well, nigga, if you think you sick, act like we already got a problem!" Budda wouldn't lose not one second of sleep if he had to knock Nardy down. He didn't like the little lying mothafucka anyway.

Before things could get further out of hand, 4-Boy came walking into the house. The front door opening drew everybody's attention. 4-Boy instantly felt the tension. He looked at all the eyes looking at him. Then saw how Budda and Nardy were standing by each other and knew he'd just interrupted them niggaz before they could do something stupid.

Brah I just left from talking to Gabby. She told me that she overheard Dooka talking to some nigga named Shark. She said Brah told the nigga that he was calling Smacks and putting him up on game about them Migos shooting up the Low last week. I asked her when was this that she heard the phone call. She said it was the day that he was going out of town to do whatever he was doing for you. I asked her was she sure and she said she was positive 'cause he told her he was making a run for you." He looked at Budda. "Anyway, I rode by the Low to see if I saw that nigga Smack's car. It's like a ghost town down in that bitch." 4-Boy knew whatever was going on before he walked in was dead now.

The possibility of P-Smacks being the last nigga to talk to Lil' Dooka was big. P-Smacks was Lil' Dooka's little brother but at the end of the day P. Smacks was a Low nigga. In reality, he was an Op. TIO was at war with 357 but the Tre-4 and the Low been beefing for years. It would be the perfect time for the Low to strike, because they were distracted with the Double Rock niggaz. And what better way for them to use an angle than to have Lil' Dooka's own brother to set him up. Everyone in the living room thought the same thing.

Mari was the one to voice it. "Y'all think that little nigga Smacks would actually set up Dooka?" He didn't pose the question to anyone in particular. He just said it out loud.

"We gotta look at it like it's a possibility no matter what. Regardless of what we may wanna believe or not. At the end of the day Smack's is a Low nigga and we gotta play it like that." Turk spoke up.

Nardy wasn't feeling the shit he was hearing. Afterall, Lil' Dooka and P. Smack was his blood. They all were so close coming up, it was like they were brothers. Nardy knew P-Smacks would never do anything to bring harm Lil' Dooka's way, and he let that shit be known.

"That shit you talking I ain't trynna hear, Turk. Smacks looks up to that nigga, Dooka. He would never cross him. He ain't about to set his own brother up. That shit is out." Nardy didn't realize that he was mugging the shit out of niggaz.

4-Boy knew exactly how Nardy felt. Before the funk started between the Top and the Bottom of the hill, he and P. Smacks were best friends. He knew P. Smacks better than anybody in the apartment. He knew there was no way in hell P-Smacks would ever turn on Lil' Dooka. The only reason he told them about what Gabby had told him was maybe Lil' Dooka had told P. Smacks something that would explain where he was at. Not because he thought P. Smacks had done some scandalous shit.

"You acting like you up in here vouching for the nigga or something." Budda knew he was shooting a dagger at Nardy. He didn't care.

"Bitch, that's still my mothafuck'n family. I am vouching for him. I know what the fuck my family would and wouldn't do. Man, you niggaz throwing me off!" Nardy stepped around 4-Boy and headed for the front door.

He wasn't going to let nobody just sit around and talk shit about his family. Homeboys or not. That shit was out. Especially Budda's punk ass. Nardy would blow his mothafuck'n head off. Let that nigga keep thinking shit was sweet.

He heard Turk and Mari calling him from inside Auntie Dee's apartment. He ignored them niggaz and kept going. As he made his way to his car, he pulled out his phone and called his cousin. Nardy had to get to the bottom of what was going on before he lost his mind.

***

Sgt. Dudley was on a mission. A mission to make the streets the way he thought they should be. And he was willing to achieve this mission by any means necessary. He pulled up to Lil' Dooka's apartment just as 4-Boy was leaving. Dudley watched him until he got in car and drove away. He waited another five minutes before getting out of the car and knocking on the front door.

Gabby was clearly in an emotional wreck. Her face was stained with mascara that had dried after streaking down her face. Evidence that she had been crying. Her hair was disheveled, and she wore a saddened look on her face. Not that Sgt. Dudley could see the sadness, he wasn't paying any attention to Gabby's face. His eyes were too busy roaming all over her little thick body. "Um... Excuse me," she snapped, getting his attention on her face and off her pussy print. "Can I help you?"

Dudley reluctantly pulled his eyes away from the front of her shorts. "I'm Sergeant Dudley." He showed her his badge. "I'm here to conduct a safety code and weapons search."

"I... I'm sorry, but DeAndre isn't here." She knew who Sgt. Dudley aka Harry Potter was. Everybody in the district knew this crooked mothafucka.

"I'm fully aware that Mr. Jordan isn't here. In fact, I am aware that he hasn't been here in days. Not since his car was found shot up and crashed in South San Francisco. The fact is, Mr. Jordan doesn't have to be present during a safety code and weapons search. Hence the nature of the search." He thought to himself that this was going to be too easy.

"I-I... Uh..." While Gabby was stuttering, Sgt. Dudley boldly stepped into the apartment. Walking right past a scared Gabby.

She should have been in her economics class today. However, she hadn't been back to school since Lil' Dooka didn't come back that night.

"So, Miss Rosales, has Mr. Jordan contacted you at all in the past couple of days?" He was putting on a pair of latex gloves as he was speaking.

She was surprised he knew her name, but she didn't say anything about it. Instead, she shook her head "no" while verbalizing the same thing.

He tried to make small talk with her as he searched the living room. But Gabby's mind was on the guns, drugs, and money that were in the apartment. Lil' Dooka told her where everything was in case of an emergency.

After he searched the living room, he went into the kitchen. Gabby's heart began racing. She thought she would die when he went to the freezer and opened the door.

"What do we have here?" Dudley pulled out three large Ziplock bags and of ecstasy pills out of the freezer along with five bottles of cough syrup that he knew they called Bo, Lean, or Syrup. The last bag he pulled out was a couple of ounces of cocaine.

He sat all the bags onto the counter very dramatically. Gabby's small heart skipped a beat every time he sat one of the bags down. After he sat the last Ziplock bag on the counter, he pulled out his handcuffs out and turned to face Gabby.

"Ma'am, please turn around and place your hands behind your back." Dudley purposely clicked the handcuffs before putting them on her to scare her.

"W-what? Hold on. That stuff ain't mine." Gabby shook her head "no" repeatedly.

"I said put your fucking hands behind your back." He walked behind her and grabbed her hands forcefully and slapped the handcuffs on her. He forced her over to a chair and made her sit down. "Now you just wait right here while I see what else you and your little Dooka got in here."

All kinds of thoughts swarmed through Gabby's mind. All she could think was the worst. It was enough drugs inside of the freezer to send her to prison for a long time. She needed to find a way out of this but how could she? What could she possibly do to prevent her entire life from going down the drain? She didn't want to spend the rest of her life inside of a prison cell. The small strand of hope and possibility melted away when he came walking out of one of the rooms carrying a couple of assault rifles. He looked at her with laughter in his eyes and shook his head.

Almost ten minutes or so later, he'd finished his search. He'd found four more handguns and a shotgun. Along with two black garbage bags filled with weed. Dudley made sure to make a show of his findings like he was auctioning shit off.

"It's unfortunate that your boyfriend is nowhere to be found. That leaves you to blame and be responsible for all these illegal items that I found inside of this apartment." He grabbed an empty chair and placed 't a few feet in front of her and took a seat in it.

"But... But... t-that stuff ain't mine. I don't even live here. I was just worried about DeAndre so I came over here." She cried.

"Such a shame too." Dudley ignored her comments and her tears. He had her right where he wanted her. "Nice pretty girl like yourself, going to college, doing good. Got your whole life ahead of you. Well, you had your whole life ahead of you. But you threw all of that away behind some dirt bag. It's enough drugs on that counter alone to get you life in prison. And them two modified assault weapons will ensure the Feds will come and see you. That's another life sentence. And you can bet your little pretty ass it won't be somewhere nice either. It'll be some women's federal facility over there in Dublin where all the guards and even that new warden is over there raping the girls. Nice, pretty, little Mexican thang like you, they'll probably be raping you every single day. Two, three times a day."

The horror of those words absolutely terrified Gabby. She couldn't imagine being raped repeatedly by some cold-hearted prison guards. A vision of her helplessly sprawled out naked on the floor in some shower stall entered her mind.

"P-Please..." she whispered. "Please, no ... Please, you got to help me."

Dudley stood up and called behind her chair. The Viagra that he took while he was parked out front watching 4-Boy leave had already kicked in. As he placed his hands on her trembling shoulders, he felt like a wolf inside of a chicken coop. He greedily licked his chops.

"Now, Gabriella, tell me why I should help someone like you out. Look out for you when you clearly haven't been looking out for yourself? Huh?" He thrust his cock up against her back as he started rubbing her shoulders.

Gabby understood now. She couldn't believe she allowed herself to be played. She felt so naive. But what could she do? She knew he was right. The drugs and guns would get her a life sentence, no doubt. After a full, thorough search and they found the money, that would all but guarantee that. She unfortunately didn't see no other way. She had to go along.

"Please… I'll do anything, just please help me," she cried at the thought of what she had to do.

His hands made their way down from her shoulders to her breast. Dudley fondled her breast. Thanking his lucky stars that he was finally going to fuck her young, sweet ass. He had been wanting to fuck her ever since she was in high school. He used to park his car by the school and jack off while he watched her at track practice. The site of her young plump ass running around in her tiny little shorts drove him insane.

He leaned down and whispered softly into her ear. "Of course, I can help you….." He kissed and licked her earlobe. "But you're going to have to help me too. Okay?"

Her mind screamed, *No, it's not okay, mothafucka!* but a soft "okay" escaped her lips.

Dudley smiled. He took the handcuffs off her wrist. "That's a good girl." With expert precision, he removed her top. Her plump, round titties were the prettiest he'd ever seen. Her big, juicy nipples were calling him. "Yes, yes, that's it. They're so beautiful."

He bent down and took one of her tits into his mouth. Gabby cringed. She felt like a thousand bugs were crawling all over her body. Dudley on the other hand, he was in heavenly bliss. The feel of his tongue running over her nipple was priceless. He mistook her groans of disgust for moans of pleasure. This encouraged him to continue. And he did, sucking each tit for a few minutes.

Tears rolled down her face.

He stood up and unzipped his pants, pulling his little dick out. He looked down at her and told her, "Now if you suck my cock good, when you're done, I'm going to see how sweet that little pussy of yours is, and maybe, just maybe, I'll forget that you were here when I came today. Now come on, baby, and suck this cock." He pressed it to her lips.

Gabby was reluctant to open her lips. She kept them closed for a few moments. He kept pressing the tip of his dick to her lips. Precum spilled onto her lips. She didn't want to. She couldn't, but she had to. Her lips trembled as she barely parted her lips. That was all Dudley needed. He forced his little hard dick into her mouth, causing her to bite her lip in the process.

Salty tears mixed with the coppery taste of blood was all she could taste as he thrust his hips back and forth, ramming his dick in and out of her mouth.

Gabby sat there frozen, silently crying.

"Ssss, that's it, that's it, you little spic bitch. Suck that mighty white cock." He looked down, watching his dick as it disappeared and reappeared.

Her mouth was sizzling hot. He had waited for this moment for so long. He wasn't seeing twenty-year-old Gabby, he was seeing that fourteen-year-old who used to bend over facing away from the bleachers that he sometimes hid under. That's who was sucking his dick. Thinking about her big breast even at fourteen straining against the material of her too small, thin gym t-shirt made him explode.

Gabby groaned loudly in disgust. The taste of his salty semen was repulsive. She couldn't help it. Her gag reflex caused her to choke and cough. This made her bite down on his dick. The pleasure of his orgasm was instantly replaced with pain. He howled and doubled over. Gabby jumped up. She didn't mean to bite his shit, but she knew that didn't matter. She'd fucked up and he was certainly going to be pissed as soon as the pain subsided.

She looked around franticly trying to find her top. She needed to get her shit and get the fuck out of there. Gabby finally saw her top over on the counter next to one of the Ziplock bags. She quickly grabbed it and put it on while she rushed to the back room to grab her purse and her keys. Dudley was on the ground crying and mumbling to himself. Gabby didn't bother trying to make out what he was saying. She ran right past him.

On her way out of the room with her shit in her hands, Gabby didn't notice Dudley was no longer on the floor. By the time she realized he was gone, it was too late. Dudley's fist crashed into the side of her jaw. The blow knocked her off her feet.

"Little stupid bitch!" He kicked Gabby in her stomach. "I tried to be nice to your nigger loving spic ass." He kicked her repeatedly as he taunted her. "This is what you wanted all along huh, bitch!"

He kicked her like a soccer player in her face. Blood instantly sprayed. Dudley dropped to his knees and commenced to beating Gabby like she was a nigga. Her face was badly beaten and bruised. She wavered in and out of consciousness. All the while he ranted and mumbled incoherent shit to her. After he beat her, he snatched her shorts and top off her and violently raped her.

The Viagra kept him rigidly stiff after he released inside of her. Sweating profusely and almost out of breath, he struggled to flip her over onto her stomach. With no form of lubrication, he forced his dick into her ass and raped her again. Gabby was powerless. The pain she felt in her bleeding anus was nothing compared to the pain caused by her humiliation and fear. Combined, it was the worst pain she'd ever felt. Gabby felt further humiliation when the pain caused her to use the bathroom on herself.

Not even the smell or sight of shit coming out of her ass would detour Sgt. Dudley. He was that level of a sick, twisted, perverted fuck, like no other. He continued to fuck her asshole.

It would be a little over three hours later before Dudley would leave a naked, badly bruised, and soiled Gabby lying on the floor, barely conscious, as he stole the drugs and guns, then left.

De'Kari

Chapter 23

The old saying, "A picture is worth a thousand words," was a little off. Because a million words ran through Rick's mind as he sat in his office staring at the picture. It was taken almost thirty years ago at a RBL Posse show.

The entire gang had come out that night to celebrate their successful rise to the top of the dope game and the reign they were about to have over the streets. Twenty-something people were in the picture, some standing, some kneeling, wearing their signature colors, black and green, relishing in the memory. Those were the best times of his life. His focus was on his inner circle; Charlie, Big Ree, Vicki, Top Dollars, Twin, Cory, O'Jay and finally Dee.

Unfortunately, he couldn't look at the picture without remembering and acknowledging that the night the picture was taken, Was the last night they would ever be all together. The next night his beloved queen and wife Aliyah would be violently murdered by his so-called loved ones, and he would be framed for her murder. They'd all set him up. Twin, Vicki, Top Dollar Charlie, all of them; even Dee. The only ones who didn't take part in the betrayal that remained loyal to him, were his two top lieutenants and best friends, Cory and O'Jay.

It would take damn near eight and a half years for Cory and O'Jay to gather the full story of what happened and why. As well as to kill everyone that was involved in the betrayal and plot to cross Spank-G. All except Vickie and Dee. Once the bodies started dropping in their circle mothafuckas got scared and fled the state. Twin was the last one. They found him hiding out in N. Carolina with some Queen Pin bitch named Paula. It was hard to get to the nigga with him dealing with that bitch and her crew. But they finally got him.

Learning that his own team, his so-called family were the ones that betrayed him, hurt Spank-G to the core. But it was the game, and he was a seasoned vet in this shit. So, he chalked it up and accepted it as one of the many lessons the game taught him. Vickie and Dee's betrayal cut him deep. Vickie was Spank's ex bitch. He treated that bitch like she was the mother of the Messiah. They separated because of her infidelity, but even then, the break-up was smooth, and he still took care of her and treated her like family. Dee was not only Vickie's blood sister; she was his most entrusted lieutenant. Even after Vickie and his break-up, he still called and considered Dee his little sister.

Once the pieces of the puzzle started falling into place. It wasn't long before he realized Dee's phone call that night was just to gauge the time of his arrival so she could let Vickie know. The sound that he'd thought he heard that night as he was walking up the stairs was Vickie sneaking out of the downstairs closet, she was hiding in. She was leaving out of the back door just as he was turning on the bedroom lights. By then the police were already on the way. Dee called them two minutes after she hung up the phone on Spank. When he found this information out, he actually cried in his cell. Dee's and Vickie's level of betrayal cut him deep in his heart and his soul. Deeper than any knife or sword could ever cut.

Somebody knocked on the door. He put the picture back inside the top drawer of his desk inside the old cigar box. Where it belonged. He took a sip of the expensive cognac that was on the desk called out to whoever it was to come in. The door swung open, and Zoey Poppins came skipping and hopping into his office. She sashayed right up to the desk and plopped down in the seat across from him.

"Zoey, where in the hell yo' lil' ass been? Come waltzing up in this muthafucka like you some kind of ballerina, when you should've had yo lil' pale ass in here weeks age." If she didn't tell him something that would blow his mind. He was going to come around the desk and break his foot off inside her little white ass.

"Calm down, Daddy. A bitch has been real busy." She took a deep breath and repeated, real busy. "But I've been out there on my shit taking care of business for you. Trynna make you proud."

"Bitch, you could've still picked up a phone and tapped in!" He knew this bitch wasn't trying to play him stupid.

"Daddy, please relax, okay. Just let me tell you everything. Then you'll see, a bitch ain't have time for no phone calls."

Rick leaned back in his chair and lit one of the blunts that was on the desk. After a few good deep drags, he blew the smoke out and said, "You better have one helluva story."

That was exactly what she had, one helluva story. She told Rick everything, beginning with killing MoMo and the two niggaz that was in front of Clty's house to killing Trucho and Casper. She saved what she did to Lil' Dooka for last. She didn't have to wonder if he was proud of her or not, the look on his face answered that question. Hell, yeah, he was impressed. She handled her business and handled it well. Good thing she was on his side. Rick would hate to have to go up against the pretty little white She-Devil.

"Did I do good, Daddy?" She sounded desperate when she asked him. It was more like a plea than a question.

"You did better than good, Zoey. You did amazing, and I'm proud of you."

"This means you'll reward me?" The pleading in her tone became begging.

He looked at her tensely, before reaching down and opening his bottom drawer. Zoey knew what he was reaching for. She began to squirm in her chair. Her skirt rode up her thighs as she crossed and uncrossed her legs.

"Okay. Get yo' ass over here." He scooted his chair away from the desk.

Zoey slowly stood up. Her pussy was on fire as she made her way toward his side of the desk. Her eyes were glued to the pair of brown leather gloves that he was putting on. Her legs trembled as she stood in front of him.

"Bitch, you know what to do," he barked.

Zoey quickly laid across his knees.

Rick reached down with his leather-gloved hand and pulled her loose skirt all the way up over her ass and laid it on her back. Her plump milky white ass checks were swallowing the hot pink thong that she was wearing. He took his hand and slowly slid it over her ass rubbing one cheek before squeezing it gently and rubbing the other.

Zoey's breathing became labored. Her pussy was so wet, it completely soaked the material of her thong. Rick could clearly see the damp spot, which was spreading. Without warning, he lifted his hand in the air and brought it back down firmly on the middle of her ass cheeks. They jiggled from the force of the slap. Zoey let out a muffled cry. He did it again. This time harder than the first. Her head shot back this time as she yelped. Rick pulled the thong she was wearing off. He could see her pussy. But he ignored it. Instead, he balled up the thong and shoved it in her mouth. Then he gave her continuous spanking.

Zoey cried tears of pleasure as she orgasmed twice. Her entire ass was red by now. Her pussy was throbbing. She liked him to talk nasty to her when he spanked her. So, he did. After about thirty or so licks, he stopped the spanking and tenderly rubbed all over her ass. He spoke soothingly to her as he did. This had poor little Zoey cumming continuously. Rick could actually see the shiny fluid as it flowed out of her like nectar. He continued to rub and massage her soft ass cheeks. Zoey absolutely loved whenever Rick spanked her. It was both breathtaking and exhilarating at the same time. Because she loved it so much, it was his way of rewarding her. Ultimately what she wanted was for him to make love her. This she would never get. His love for Trina was too strong for that. But he had no problem spanking her little ass. Which he began to do some more.

When he finished, her ass was beet red and sore. Her pussy was throbbing, and she had a giant smile spread across her face. She stood up and shook her ass checks as she took the thong out of her mouth and slid it back up her legs and over her sore ass. She looked down at the puddle of her fluids that was on his lap then bent down and licked the puddle up.

***

The light pierced Dooka's eyes when he tried to open them. He flinched and closed them back. Shit his entire body hurt like fuck. Like he got hit by a cement truck. He tried to move but bolts of pain erupted in numerous places in his body at the same time. He tried to remember what happened to him, but he couldn't.

"No, no, no, no! Don't try to move, Dooka. Just lay back. Your body has been through quite a lot." Her voice was as beautiful as the sound of a musical harp.

Natty rushed to his side to assist him in any way she could. When he opened his eyes, he knew he had to be dead. In front of him was an angel. It had to be. No one on earth was that beautiful. He blinked again, this time to see if she would disappear. Maybe his mind was playing tricks on him.

She didn't disappear...

He blinked his eyes again. This time holding them closed for a moment or two. The pain was too much. At least when his eyes were closed the pain subsided some. He tried to speak but his mouth and throat were so dry all he did was choke, then cough. Which caused more pain.

"Wait a minute.... Hold on now. You've come thru too much to hurt yourself right now for no reason. Here." She grabbed a pitcher filled with water that was sitting on the nightstand next to the bed, put a straw in it and placed it in his mouth.

"Take it easy now. Be careful." She told him after he drunk almost half of the pitcher.

Finally, he released the straw with a loud smack of his lips. He was out of breath from sucking up so much water. His broad chest heaved up and down. He struggled to speak but could only manage weak, W-who?

My name is Nathalie, but you can call me Natty. That was all Lil' Dooka heard before he became lightheaded, and everything turned black.

De'Kari

Chapter 24

I'm telling you Reem them niggaz don't understand. They throwing me off with that weird shit. Niggaz ain't even focused on getting money anymore. All they wanna talk about and focus on is them Double Rock niggaz..." Lil' Nardy was at Baby Reno's grave. Drunk as fuck talking to his brotha. "Nigga, this is TIO! Tear It Off! We ain't tearing off shit on BR niggaz pockets are damn near touching and them stupid mothafuckas still just wanna worry about getting them niggaz.

He stumbled and tripped on his feet, nearly falling. He burped. Stood up and spun around on his feet. Looking around at all the grave sites like they'd just appeared out of nowhere.

"M-Mind you BR, we not even beefing with the entire Double Rock niggaz. We beefing with a couple of niggaz from Double Rock. They call themselves 357. But now that nigga Budda done come home and that nigga done declared war on all of Double Rock. That's weird B. now we gonna be waring with mothafuckas forever!"

He lifted the bottle of Hennessy that was in his hand and took a good swig. He was so drunk that he got dizzy from tilting his head backward. This time he did fall. He landed right on his ass. At that moment his stomach decided he had consumed too much alcohol. It gave a violent upheave and Nardy threw up. He turned his head to the side, but he was too slow, most of the vomit got all over the front of his Givenchy outfit.

"Damn BR I think I might be drunk," he spoke to the grave. Then he started laughing hysterically like he'd just heard the funniest joke in the world.

Nardy didn't give a fuck about being drunk. He was tired of all the dumb shit. His little bitch was about to have a baby and instead of getting his money up so he could take care of his kid he, was in the streets playing Black Ops like a fucking idiot. All because niggaz lost sight of the bigger picture. He was done. Fuck Dooka and Budda! If them niggaz wanted to run around and play like they were gangsters, that was on them. Nardy had his own plans, and they didn't involve being a broke ass nigga in the county jail fighting a murder charge. He was saying fuck the dumb shit. He was getting out.

He fumbled around in his pockets for his pack of Backwoods and a lighter. The Backwoods were filled with that Cali good. He took a blunt out and lit it. The pungent smell of the weed invaded the cool crisp air of the cemetery.

"Shit BR I'm serious man. This war shit ain't for me brah. That's why I dropped by so a nigga could tell you I love you before I get on. I'm not with this shit, brotha. And I know if you was still alive you wouldn't be with this stupid shit either. We was fly niggaz. Getting to that paper and getting to them bitches. That's what I'm get back on. Fuck Sunnydale and TIO. I'mma bout to shoot to another city. Get me a click of young niggaz and get these Benjamins...." Nardy stopped talking as a shadow fell over the gravesite and his legs.

He looked up. He was shocked to find himself looking down the barrel of a gun.

"Yeah, bitch-ass nigga, you right about that. Fuck Sunnydale and fuck TIO! This O'Hunnid, bitch!" The shooter squeezed the trigger.

When Nardy first saw the gun thousands of ways he could beg for this life came to mind. Those thoughts followed the rest of his thoughts and the brain matter that the bullets blew out o' his fucking head. Nardy flew backward and landed right next to the head stone. The shooter stood over Nardy's lifeless body and still emptied the clip into him. The way Nardy's body fell, it looked like he was taking a nap on top of the grave.

Don knew that sooner or later at least one of them mothafuckas would come and visit the grave. So, he would come and wait a few hours each day. All at different times of the day and night hoping that he would catch one. He had already been posted in his hiding spot when Nardy first approached the grave. He wasn't gonna kill him at the gravesite at first out of respect, but when he got to crying like a lil' bitch and talking, he said fuck it. Only reason he didn't kill Nardy right away was out of respect for BR. Afterall, the kid wasn't even in the beef. In Don's mind at least now, the kid would have some company.

He spit a loogey on Nardy's body before turning and walking away.

***

Dell was on his way back to the hood. He, Murda and XO had just slid through Sunnydale and knocked a couple of niggaz down. Fuck pulling skits. Mothafuckas were on straight bodying-shit mode. They were going to lay low for a couple of hours. Enough time to give homicide a chance to do their thing, then they were going to double back and knock some more shit down. Them Sunnydale niggaz won't be able to live, get money, or fucking move until 357 Mobb tell them bitches they can. It was murder season, and the killers were out hunting.

His cell phone started ringing just as he was passing Candlestick Park. "Yeah, what's up," he answered, not recognizing the number.

"I-is this Dell?" The voice was a female, and he could tell she was nervous.

"Shorty, you called my phone, but you don't know my voice. Who is this? And what you want, ma?" He came to a stop at a red light.

"I don't know you, but you and I need to talk."

"Is that right? Well Shorty why don't we start with you at least telling me your name." The light turned green, and he was getting ready to turn until what she said made him stop in the middle of the street.

"My name is Rayna. I hear you've been trying to get hold of me."

"Hell yeah! I've been trynna get ahold of you. I found your number inside of my little brother's phone. In fact, you were the last person he spoke to. I'm hoping maybe you can tell me something about my little brother or that night that we don't already know.

Something that might tell us what happened to him." He held his breath and waited.

He knew that being direct would either appeal to her womanly instincts like caring, nourishing, helping, or it would send her off running as far away and as fast as she could go.

"I was with him that night," she blurted out.

Dell wasn't expecting to hear that. He just kept quiet. She was talking and he was going to let her talk as much as she wanted. She finally paused and then she gave him the name and room number to her motel in South City and told him that they should talk in person. Then she hung up in his face.

Dell didn't realize he had stopped in the middle of an intersection. He hadn't even heard the car horns honking around him. As soon as Rayna hung up, he flipped a U-turn and headed toward the freeway.

He was cautious as he pulled into the parking lot. His .44 Desert Eagle rested nicely on his lap. He was more than aware that he could be walking into a trap. His gut told him that wasn't the case. He drove around the parking lot looking for both the room number and anything that didn't fit. When he found the room, he parked in an empty space right in front of it. If something was waiting for him, he would meet it head on.

He didn't want to scare the girl, so he tucked the Desert Eagle in his waste before knocking on the door. If an ambush was coming it would most likely be coming from behind him. So, he turned around and faced the parking lot and waited for the door to open. It didn't take long. Once he heard it open, he turned around and came face to face with the barrel of a snub-nose 38. He looked pass the barrel and into a cute face and a set of terrified eyes.

"I mean damn Shorty. If you called me out here to tell me you the one that killed my little brother or had something to do with him getting killed, then go ahead and pull the trigger. Cause if you don't I will. But if that ain't the case, then put that away cause I ain't yo enemy.

She dropped her eyes to the ground, her bottom lip trembled. The gun in her hand began to shake. For a split second, Dell was nervous that she'd accidently pull the trigger and blow his head off. Tears rolled down her pretty face as she slowly lowered her arm. Dell took a deep breath and then took a risk. He slowly reached out and took her into his arms. Giving her a much-needed hug.

"I didn't do it." She cried out into his chest. "I swear I didn't have anything to do with it. I-I, I t-think I loved your brother."

Dell stood there for a minute holding her while she cried. He was nervous and felt exposed with his back to the parking lot like it was, even though he kept his head on swivel. When he figured he chanced being exposed, out in the open long enough, he ushered her into the room.

He guided her to the couch and had her sit down. Then, even with her in the middle of a full fledge break down, he left her there and did a full security check of the room. For all Dell knew, the little bitch could've been an Oscar performance giving mothafucka. He didn't need no surprises. There was one bedroom with a closet, a bathroom, a small hallway with another closet and a small kitchenette. It didn't take no time for him to clear the area and return to Rayna. She was still seated on the couch crying her heart out.

Dell noticed that he'd forgotten to lock the door. So, he walked over to it and locked it. Out of habit he peeked outside through the curtains and checked the perimeter. Everything looked normal so he walked over to the couch and sat next to Rayna.

Given that he didn't know her, he had no idea how fragile she was. Because of this, he didn't try to rush her. He sat patiently. For some reason his heart went out to the young lady. He could sense that her pain was genuine.

There was a box of Kleenex on the coffee table. He reached and picked it up. He took a nice wad out and handed them to her. She mumbled a thank you as she took the tissue and wiped her eyes and then blew her nose.

She was trying to pull herself together. It was hard because Dell looked so much like Wes from his facial features and build, down to the same ducktail. Wes was just a little taller than Dell. But even a blind bitch could tell they were brothers.

Looking into her face Dell could see her features better. She really was a real cutie pie. Just the type of girl his brother went for. The cream of the crop. Rayna was a show-stopper fa'sho. Don could also tell from looking closely at her, that she wasn't green to the game. She might not have been a full seasoned vet, but she wasn't no rookie either. He made a mental note of that.

Finally, she got herself together enough, she felt. She took his hands into hers and held on to them as she told on the complete story. She started with the very first time they met at the club, and she finished with the tragic way that last night ended. Dell thought she was done but when he started to speak, she began another story. It was one of intuition, reflection, and a little detective work. And it began with a phone call from a friend in need of help. A friend who would turn on and betray the very friend that she called on for help.

Having all this time to think, rethink and go over everything that transpired that night. Rayna was positive that Alyssa set her and Wes up. Alyssa got Wes killed and stole Rayna's happiness. Revenge was a dish best served cold. Well, Rayna thought it wasn't cold enough.

Chapter 25

Rick had been calling C1ty's phone almost to the point where it felt like Rick was sweating him. C1ty would never let any nigga feel that he was hiding from them. That's why he decided to pop up at Rick's spot and have a talk with him. Shit had been crazy the past couple of days. They were on All Gas No Brakes Mode for the last two weeks. Today was the first day they had to breathe, and he decided it was the perfect time to holla at the old man.

Pulling into the long wrap-around driveway his phone vibrated. When he stopped the car C1ty decided to check his phone before getting out. He had a text message from Dell telling him that they needed to hook up a.s.a.p. He sent a reply letting his brother know that he would hit him up in thirty minutes to see where he wanted to link up at.

The front door to the mansion opened as he was tucking his phone back into his pocket. C1ty looked from behind the tints of his ride as a bad ass white bitch came walking out of the door. She had a body like Krystal from the Black Ink Crew New York television show. Something about her was throwing him off but he couldn't figure out what it was. He watched and studied everything about her. That big ass booty kept distracting him.

She was a sexy little mothafucka. Yet, the vibes he was getting weren't good vibes at all. So, he ignored the bitches body and focused on her face. The moment she opened the driver's door of the baby Benz something jumped out at him. He had to lean forward in his seat to make sure. She was climbing in the driver's seat, disappearing from view. All kinds of alarms went off in his head as he saw the confirmation. Her hair was died red on one side and blue on the other. His mind went back to a couple weeks before.

"Aye yo. Before I forget. I did some digging into what actually happened to them Gas Nation niggaz that were rolling on security that night." It Was XO who called this out.

"Okay. What's up?" C1ty looked over at his cousin.

"Word is, it was a white bitch that got them niggaz," he responded.

"A white bitch?"

"Yeah, some white bitch with blue and red hair ...... Yeah, some white bitch with blue and red hair blue and red hair...... blue and red hair... blue and red."

That shit kept replaying over and over in his head, as he watched the bitch drive away. True, just because the bitch had dyed hair didn't mean she was the bitch that killed the two niggaz in front of his spot. But the odds of having two white bitches on the same side of the city, with that sane description both running in the same circle. That shit wasn't likely. A nigga had a better chance getting struck in the ass by lightning, surviving, and going on to win the mothafuck'n lottery.

He didn't have time to reflect on that shit. He got out the car and went and rang the doorbell. Ebony answered the door. She greeted him and let him in the house. He followed her to her uncle's study. She knocked on the door, then turned and left. C1ty waited a couple seconds until Rick called out for him to enter. He did.

Rick was seated behind his desk going over one of his many business ledgers. Miles Davis played the saxophone smoothly in the background of a softly lit room. The soft light and jazz music always helped Rick transform from the gangsta he did as Spank-G to the business mindset of Rick.

He wrote something down inside of his ledger, then set the pen inside of the book and closed it.

"Well, well, well. I was beginning to get a little nervous. It's not like you not to answer your phone and obviously you're not dead. So, what's going on?" he asked C1ty as he leaned back in the big leather chair. He crossed his hands of over his abdomen.

C1ty didn't wait for Rick to invite him to have a seat. He sat down on his own. "Shit. My bad about the phone situation. Shit's just been really hot lately and I figured it was best not to be dealing with the phone. For everybody's safety."

"I've noticed the body count has been climbing. Even the police have begun to beef up their patrols. How's that look for our business?"

"Business won't stop. We're still going to stick to the plan. It's just the next job is gonna be postponed a couple of weeks." C1ty didn't know how Rick was going to take hearing that. But it is what it is.

Before Rick had a chance to respond to C1ty. The doors to the study came open, getting both of their attention. "Daddy, I'm sorry, I forgot to give you..." Zoey Poppins came walking into the study with a Hermes carry bag draped over her shoulders. She stopped in mid-sentence and mid-stride at the sight of C1ty. "Oh! I'm sorry, Daddy, I didn't realize you had company. I just got a little way away and realized I didn't give you this." She gestured to the bag.

Rick noticed the way the two of them looked at each other. Yet, he didn't say nothing about it. "It's okay, baby. Come on in and bring it over here."

Zoey crossed the study while observing C1ty. When she was leaving the house, she knew somebody was behind the tinted windows of the Camaro watching her. She could feel their eyes on her as she walked to her Benz and hopped in. She didn't like the feelings she felt at the time. She played it off real smooth, knowing that she was going to double back and pop up on that ass, Zoey Poppins style.

She walked over and gave Rick the bag. For a moment she and C1ty made eye contact. He gave her a small smile and a slight head nod. There was nothing warm in the smile. Zoey merely winked at C1ty. He knew this was the bitch. He could feel it in his bones. What he didn't know was their angle. He didn't know what the fuck was going on. But he was going to find out.

Rick took the bag and sat it down next to his feet. He watched Zoey walk out and close the door.

"Do you think changing the timetable on things is a good idea? Especially with all that's going on?" He didn't bother commenting on Zoey or her interruption.

"Won't know if it's a good idea or not until it's all said and done. But it's not negotiable. I've already decided, we decided that this rather small distraction has carried on so long because we've virtually ignored it. None of us likes a nuisance, so it's time to deal with it and end it once and for all. Shouldn't take no longer than a week from now."

Having these little niggaz rob them banks was only a means to real them in. Turned out to be a helluva idea. A lucrative one too. But at the end of the day, it was a means to an end. Rick didn't want to let the money sidetrack him. Getting all of them little mothafuckas to go to war with each other had been the plan all along. Therefore, it wouldn't make any sense to try and change C1ty's mind. He barely could conceal the smile that was dying to spread across his face. Everything was going beautifully according to plans.

"Well considering the loss that you took. I can understand the importance in dealing with things accordingly and with efficiency. Just make sure you keep your eyes open and stay two steps ahead of your enemy. If you need anything you know all you gotta do is say something.'"

"It's good big homie. I appreciate the offer, but we got this, Trust. C1ty rose out of his chair.

Rick rose also. The two men shook hands and on cue, Ebony was there to escort C1ty out. He swore, if the bitch didn't have ESP, there had to be live video feed cameras inside of the study. Rick never called anybody or pushed any buttons, yet every time they were done with a meeting, Ebony popped up ready to escort him out. C1ty didn't say shit though. He kept all his thoughts to himself as he followed her through the house. He enjoyed watching her ass shake as she walked in front of him. Just cause he was faithful to Genesis didn't mean he couldn't enjoy looking at a nice ass whenever he saw one. And the way Ebony walked C1ty knew that shit was fire.

Ebony didn't close the door until C1ty made it to his Camaro. When he opened the driver's door he looked up. She waived at him, and he threw her a nod. He jumped in the car and drove off. He waited until he was a couple of blocks away before he picked up his phone and called Dell.

He answered right away, "Speak on it."

"Yo, what's up, bro. I just finished taking care of some business with the OG. I'm trynna see what's good with you though," C1ty replied.

"Shit, I just made it to the spot. So I'mma 'bout to fry up a couple of burgers. We need to hook up I got some shit I need to drop on you."

"Say less. Fry me up a couple of them joints. I'm on my way there right now. Cause bro I got some shit I got to hit you with as well." He hung up the phone and headed to C-Block.

The smell of the hamburgers made C1ty's mouth water as soon as he came through the front door. He was glad that he told Dell to fry up a couple for him, because he was fucking starving. Both CJ and Don were sitting on the couch in the living room each chowing down on a big ass burger and fries.

"Shit big brah, the way you got it smelling in here niggaz need to think about opening up some kind of food joint. If this shit taste half as good as it smells, nigga we gonna be rich ass fuck." C1ty called out to Dell.

"Trust. This shit taste way better than it smells C1ty." CJ confirmed. Talking around a mouth full of food.

Don couldn't say nothing, shit was too good. He simply nodded his head up and down in agreement.

"Little brah you got perfect timing." Dell came walking out the kitchen holding a plate with four juicy patties stacked two by two with what looked like three different kinds of cheese smothering them. "Lettuce and shit is on the table. You gotta dress these bitches yo'self."

"Big brah, these bitches look so good, thanks. A nigga bout to knock a patch out these bitches." C1ty grabbed the plate from Dell and headed straight for the table to put his double cheeseburgers together.

Dell came back out of the kitchen with a big plate of fries and another plate with his burgers on it. He sat across the table from

C1ty and began dressing his burgers. He talked while he made his sandwiches.

Turns out that the little Mexican bitch that CJ and XO came across a little while back that gave us the info on that Auntie Dee bitch, she was the one that set up Wes." That statement got all their attention. "That bitch that I'd been trying to get ahold of fucked around and got ahold of me. The one who's number was the last number that lil' brah called that night." Dell took a big bite out of his burger and told the three of them everything that Rayna told him about that night and the shit that she figured out later about that night.

When he finished with that, he shared with them all the shit Rayna told him about the TIO Click. Who lived where, who drove what, who be who. He went on to say that Rayna was happy to tell it all because Lil' Dooka and them niggaz stole her heart and only chance at happiness. She wanted them to avenge her broken heart.

XO was the first one to speak up. "So, when we moving on them niggaz?"

C1ty spoke up, "Somebody call Murda and XO and tell them niggaz to get over here."

"Their already on their way. Once them two popped by and I knew you were on the way, I called them niggaz and told them to slide thru," Dell told him.

"Then we on this shit ASAP as soon as they get here." C1ty picked up a handful of fries and shoved them in his mouth.

Like two magicians, Dell and Murda came walking through the front door right at that exact moment. As quick as he could, Dell ran everything down to them. Everybody agreed that they shouldn't waste time with the information they had. Tonight, they would strike.

After they were done discussing everything that Dell had found out from Rayna and mapping out their plans for tonight's attacks. C1ty told them about his trip to O.G. Rick's mansion and the exchange with the white bitch with the red and blue hair. No one believed in the possibility of there being two different white bitches tied to all of this shit. The bitch that C1ty saw at the O.G.'s spot had to be the same white bitch that killed the Gas Nation niggaz. The shit didn't add up or make sense. They would just have to sit down once this business with the little niggaz was finished and figure this shit out.

De'Kari

Chapter 26

"Bitch, you stupid. I wish I would let some faggot ass Double Rock niggaz keep me from getting my money. How you sound? Nigga, instead of talking that slick shit, why don't yo' hoe ass just tell a nigga that you need some money. You broke mothafucka," Budda joked in the phone.

"Bitch, I can't be broke, when I got yo' mama out on the blade and giving me her SSI check," the nigga Weezy shot back at him.

These two niggaz loved each other more than brothas. They talked shit and cracked jokes all the time without anyone ever getting offended or taking shit personal. That's how close they were. Weezy was currently inside of Kern Valley State Prison in his cell talking to Budda on his cell phone.

"Yeah, yo ass gotta send somebody out there to collect the money from all the niggaz that played yo dumb ass." They both laughed some more. "But on the real, as soon as we get off the phone, I'm gonna have Bae drop a lil' sum'n, sum'n in your Cash App or in the other account."

"Nah, bitch, drop twenty stacks, with yo' chimney ass," Weezy joked.

"Keep talking, bitch, and I'll tell her to drop ten." Budda was around the corner from his house. He was tired as fuck. They'd been going four days straight knocking down any nigga that they found on Fitzgerald that looked to be over the age of twelve. They even went inside the Alice Griffin Housing Projects a couple of times. Catching niggaz slipping and making an example out of them. Their body count for the four days was eleven. Mothafuckas were getting the picture. His plan was to go home, get some food, some much-needed sleep, spend time with his daughter and be right back in the field in two days. There was no plan to let up.

"Yeah, yeah, whatever nigga. It's almost count time. Let me get off this jack, before them bitches catch me slipping."

"Yeah, alright. Hit me up tomorrow, nigga. Luv you." Budda hung up just as he was pulling up to the stop sign at the corner of his street. He made sure to text his queen about sending the money first thing in the morning in case she was sleep when he got in.

The sound of screeching tires caught his attention. There was no need to look up. Budda knew what time it was. He slapped that bitch in reverse and smashed the gas. The big AMG responded immediately but he only went a few feet before he crashed into the grill of a big Chevy Duramax. He quickly threw the Benz back into drive and stomped down on the gas.

Gunfire erupted!

Bullets were hitting the Benz from every angle, except the passenger side. Budda knew it was helpless. They had him boxed in. He wasn't about to get up out of there. The hot bullets that hit his body had him enraged. He upped the big Desert Eagle that was resting under his leg and started shooting back. His shots were wild. Glass from the shattered window flew in his eyes. Shit, he didn't know where the mothafuckas were that were shooting him. He just fired in whatever direction a bullet hit him from.

He tried to duck low and shoot. A bullet crashed into his jaw, snapping his head back and shattering his jawbone. He couldn't stay boxed in like this, he told himself. If he did, he would be dead in seconds. Budda fired a few more rounds and dove toward the passenger door. Somehow, he managed to get it open without catching another bullet. He pulled his body through the open door. Budda had enough energy in him to at least take a few of these bitches with him if he was going out.

He ignored the fact that he was coughing up a lot of blood and tightened his grip on the handle. He took a deep breath and started to push himself up off the ground. A foot came crashing into his face. Busting his mouth and knocking four teeth out. He was so dizzy from the blow that he didn't realize all the gunshots had stopped.

Budda was on the floor. Blood gushed out of his mouth and ran down the front of his shirt. He was barely conscious. Hanging on to his life by a slim thread. In his blurred vision he could barely make out the image of C1ty standing in front of him in all black.

Straight Beast Mode 2

Instinctively Budda lifted his hand. He aimed at C1ty's silhouette, but his hand was empty. The Desert Eagle went sliding out of his hands when C1ty kicked him in the face. Budda didn't realize he wasn't holding the gun. He kept pulling his finger like he was shooting the gun.

"You should've stayed yo' ass in jail, bitch!" C1ty angrily spit as he pulled the trigger, shooting Budda in the face at point blank range. Budda's brain along with the back of his head flew back inside the Benz, landing on the passenger set seat.

"So much for their fucking Messiah," C1ty said as he turned around and walked back to the Durango.

***

"Well, Dee, they say that bitch revenge, is a real cold mothafucka. Something about it being a dish best served cold or some shit. I can't even lie, that bitch is feeling real good right now. I thought I was robbed of my personal satisfaction when I couldn't personally kill the other members of the team. But you know what? Seeing you guys' kids die because of the betrayal and fuck shit that y'all did was beyond anything a nigga could ask for."

"Truthfully, I never expected them lil' niggaz to kill you. Bitch, I had something personal planned for your disloyal, conniving ass. But shit doesn't always go as planned. Tell me something, Dee, whatever happened to *Death Before Dishonor*, huh, bitch? That was our fucking motto. But you rat mothafuckas betrayed me and set me up. You killed my fucking queen—"

"Rick, baby, it wasn't even like that." Vickie interrupted him.

"Bitch, shut the fuck up!" He backhanded her in the face, knocking her over. She let out a yelp as her body sprawled out across the cold damp grass that covered Auntie Dee's grave site.

"B- But it was supposed to be us. Instead, y-you, you married that bitch and forgot all about me!" Vickie cried.

The moment he heard Vickie refer to Aliyah as a bitch, he kicked her hard in the stomach like he would've a nigga.

"Bitch, didn't I tell you to shut the fuck up!" He kicked her again. This time, Vickie threw up.

"We was supposed to be fucking family!" he shouted at Dee's grave. "We got them RBL niggaz out of the way. Them Big Block niggaz didn't even want it with us. Everything was perfect for a full-scale full city take over. Even the Lake View and Filmore niggaz was ready to get with the fucking program. Bitch, do you know what the fuck we could've done with the whole city united? I'd just had a meeting with the Shrimp Bay. For the first time, even the Asians were standing behind us. The whole team would've had more fucking millions than they know what to do with.

"But it's okay though. Now I see an even bigger picture. That's right, an even more lucrative way to make more money. And it's all legal. All I gotta do is finish tying up a few loose strands. Taking care of a few scraggly, disloyal weasel-like mothafuckas that know too much. Like this sniveling yellow bitch right here." Rick reached down and grabbed Vickie by a handful of hair

She cried and begged him not to hurt her, but Rick wasn't listening. As far as he was concerned, she could cry and scream all night. They were the only ones at the cemetery.

"Rick. Please, Daddy! Please, I'll do anything just please don't. Please don't hurt me, Daddy. Please!" Vickie was begging for dear life.

Humiliating the bitch would actually be the cherry on top, he figured. Make her feel small and ashamed like he felt once word got out that he was betrayed and set up by his own family. The same family he'd bled and killed for.

He pulled his dick out of his pants. "You'll do whatever huh?" Before Vickie could answer he shoved his dick into her mouth. She started sucking immediately. She had his limp dick rock hard in under four seconds. Rick had forgotten how good Vickie could suck a dick. It was one of the things he loved about her while they were together. He couldn't help getting turned on while watching his dick disappeared behind her thick lips.

Vickie was a bad bitch. That goes without saying since she used to be his bitch. She was a beautiful Latin mixed with Samoan with a helluva body. She had the big titties like her sister, although Dee's were bigger. But she had what Dee didn't, a big ass booty. Vickie was working with 44/46 inches easily.

Rick couldn't help it. The temptation was too strong. He made Vickie turn around and pull her yoga pants down. The site of her big ole yellow booty made him lick his lips. He got down on his knees behind her and jammed his dick into her hot pussy. Vickie looked at her sister's head stone and said a silent prayer asking Dee to forgive her for what they were doing on top of her grave.

Rick was grudge-fucking the shit out of her. His thighs smacked against her big ass cheeks so hard it sounded like someone was clapping.

Vickie couldn't help it. The dick was so good she began throwing it back at him. She moaned loudly, no longer concerned with holding back her enjoyment of the pleasure. When she reached her orgasm, she started pounding her fist on the grass. She was telling Rick how good the dick was, but he wasn't listening. The sight of her golden yellow ass cheeks clapping like this was a music video was fucking his mind up. He reached behind him.

"Come on, bitch. Make that pussy swallow this dick!" In response, Vickie threw that shit back as hard as she could.

Another orgasm was building inside of her. She felt Rick's dick swell inside of her. His thrust became sporadic. The tale, tale signs that he was about to explode. Vickie reached between her legs and lightly pinched her clitoris. That did it. She felt like a spaceship launched inside of her pussy. Her whole body began shaking like she was having a seizure.

Rick felt the nutt building. He raised his arm like he was reaching to grab a handful of hair. That big ole yellow booty had him hypnotized. His stomach tightened and his balls erupted, sending a stream of hot semen into her. At that exact moment he pulled the trigger of the big .45 he'd just grabbed from behind.

Vickie never felt the bullet enter her brain. She was dead before her nerves could register that happened the explosion in the head. The front of her face was joined with half of her brain and brain matter. All of it sprayed across the head stone.

Rick stood up and pissed on Vickie's dead body and on Auntie Dee's grave. When he finished, he turned to leave. He left Vickie's partially naked dead body laid out on top of her sister's grave with her face blown off.

Chapter 27

Sergeant Dudley returned to his desk with a puzzled look on his face. He had just come from visiting Detective Gillispie over in Homicide. He was trying to see how much evidence she had collected in the case involving the prostitute found raped in the alley. He also wanted to know what angle she was going with the case, as far as a suspect was concerned. Sgt. Dudley knew he didn't kill the black bitch but that would be hard to explain considering he'd left a nutt sack full of semen inside of her when he raped her.

It wasn't Gillispie's investigation that him baffled. It was the fact that she told him that she was no longer on the case. According to Det. Gillispie the investigation had been taken over by the Feds. He could manipulate the case from within if Gillispie was still on. He could even destroy or alter evidence, but with the Feds dealing with it, he felt like someone was driving a semi up his ass.

To make matters worse the station was full today. Everyone was making sure they crossed their I's and dotted all of their T's before the annual audit tomorrow. The captain had been breathing down everybody's neck for the last month or so. It seemed to Dudley that there was a bunch of whispering going on in the office.

Dudley looked across his desk to Det. Morgan's empty chair. He noticed that it seemed that she was never around lately. On a few occasions he called her on her cell. Each time she'd just tell him that she was caught up with some personal shit or checking up on one kind of lead or another. Right now, he wished she was at her desk. Morgan always stayed up on the latest news and gossip that was going on inside of the precinct. Dudley didn't know why his stomach was uneasy, but it was. Or why he felt like every time he looked up someone was staring at him.

He couldn't take this shit no more. He had to get out of the station and clear his head, maybe jack another drug dealer. Dudley was running low on his Coke, that shit he took out of Lil' Dooka's apartment was almost gone. He needed some more.

As he was putting the finishing touches on his latest case, he noticed the room had gotten extremely quiet. Dudley's instincts started screaming. His curiosity got the best of him. He looked up from the report. What he saw made his heart drop out of his chest. His partner Morgan was dressed in a black business suit with a long trench coat. Next to her on her left was Captain Harris. On Morgan's right was a middle-aged white dude he had never seen before. Next to him was Sergeant Rochelle Watkins. She was the head of Internal Affairs. A flock of about ten unformed officers followed closely behind the four of them. All of them were headed directly for him.

He forced himself not to look away. Even though he'd done more crooked shit than Denzel Washington did in *Training Day*. The only thing his mind could think about was the black bitch he'd raped in that alley way over in Potrero Hills.

When the entourage reached his desk, it was Captain Harris who spoke. "Sergeant Dudley, I need for you to hand me your badge and your weapon."

"What? For what? W-what's going on?" He tried hard not to let his fears show.

"Sergeant you are under arrest now...."

"Under arrest? He cut the captain off. He looked to the rookie, his partner, "Morgan what the fuck is this?"

Morgan took a step forward. "My name is Special Agent Lawanda Price FBI, and you are under arrest you piece of shit ......" Dudley tried to interrupt her, but she wouldn't have it.

"Thanks to a two-year investigation you piece of shit we got you for bribery, extortion, planting evidence, rape, forced sexual assault, murder and a laundry list of other things." She looked at the guy that Sergeant Dudley didn't know. "Cuff this piece of shit Jack and get him the fuck outta here.

Agent Jackson Snatched Dudley roughly up from his seat. Dudley began to protest but a punch to the midsection from Agent Jackson quieted all that.

The fucking FBI. A two-year investigation. Dudley had done so much in that time period he could get the death penalty. Morgan a fucking fed. He couldn't believe it. Rather he believed it or not. Reality was a bitch and she just fucked him.

***

Murda was in his element. He slipped through the window soundless like some evil phantom, or shadow. His eyes could see in the pitch black off the house just as good as they could in the broad day light. He made his way swiftly and stealthily through the house toward the front door. He was almost to the door when he noticed two bodies on the couch sleeping. He changed course and headed for the couch. Along the way Murda pulled out a long scary looking knife with serrated edges. He crept toward the couch and made sure neither body would wake up again.

He made it to the front door and opened it. Letting the Hands of Hell into the house. XO asked him what took him so long to open the door. Murda pointed at the two bodies lying on the couch with their throats cut. Reco would never get the chance to yell TIO again.

Dell, Don, and CJ were already creeping through the house looking for their victims. Dell and Don both went up the stairs. The thick carpet prevented the stairs from creaking under their weight. The two brothers had their guns out and ready. There were two rooms and a bathroom upstairs. The door to the bathroom was open making things a lot easier. Each brother headed toward a door.

CJ ignored the stairs and headed toward the one lone room at the back of the house. He knew the door on his left was the bathroom. He crept right past it. When he got to the bedroom, he turned the knob and let the door swing in. Gun raised and ready, he stepped thru the doorway into an empty room. He scanned the room twice to make sure. The clicking sound of a gun being chambered behind him made CJ freeze.

The sound of the gun, in the still silent of the night was like cannon fire. The first shot was followed by two more. CJ looked down at his shirt in disbelief. There was nothing there. Instead, when he turned around the holes, he'd expected to find in his chest were actually in the chest of the nigga who had crept out of the bathroom with a Glock .23 in his hand Turk had a shocked look on his face and a blank stare in his eyes as he dropped to his knees. Murda was behind him holding the big Desert Eagle.

The loud gun shots woke 4-Boy up out of his sleep. First thing he did was reach for the Tech 9 that he kept on the nightstand. He scrambled out of bed naked with the Tech 9 in his hand. The little bitch that was in bed with him was still high. She had no idea what was going on. The bedroom door came crashing open, 4-Boy spun around, raising the Tech as he did.

Too late!

A swarm of chopped up pennies and hot buck shot tore into his body lifting him off his feet. Don walked over to get as close as he could to 4-Boy who landed on top of the bitch. Don stood there and repeatedly jacked the shotgun off and filling both 4-Boy and the bitch with everything that was in the gun. Blood, gunpowder, and feathers were flying around everywhere in the room. Don left the room and went to go check on Dell.

Tatiyana was riding the fuck out of TG in the reverse cowgirl position. She did this thing where she leaned forward toward his knees and started twerking on his dick. She was doing the Matrix on his dick. He smacked her hard on her massive ass cheeks at the exact time the first gunshot went off. So, he grabbed the Glock .40 that was under his pillow. He was bringing it up as the room door got kicked in.

Tatiyana lifted up to see who had barged in the room just as TG was squeezing the trigger. Instead of catching Dell off guard, he blew a hole the size of Mississippi through Tatiyana's head. TG kept squeezing the trigger, sending bullets everywhere except for where they needed to go. Dell dropped down on one knee as soon as the first shot rang out. While TG was still shooting, Dell crept around to the side of the bed when he got to the head of the bed he raised up.

His gun was level with TG's head. "Peak-a-Boo, Nigga!"

He squeezed the trigger and knocked the far side of TG's head off. A noise at the entrance of the hallway drew his attention. He swung his arm toward the door just as Don's face came into view. Dell stood up and they made their way downstairs. The information that Rayna had given to Dell paid off beautifully. All the main hittas for TIO were dead. The only one remaining was Lil' Dooka.

De'Kari

Chapter 28
7:04 a.m.

"Thank you, Pam. The neighborhoods of Excelsior, Visitacion Valley, and Bayview Hunters Point, especially the section known as Double Rock where the Alice Griffith Housing Projects are located, have been stricken with a wave of gun violence and murder that is reminiscent of the 1980's epidemic that resulted from the drug wars of the Crack epidemic."

"Just last night in a string of shootings that stretched from these districts all the way to the Potrero Hill District, nine people were left dead. Six of those people that were killed were found right here in this two-story house behind me on Blythedale Avenue. Our sources tell us that in the twilight hours of last night masked gunmen stormed this house like an elite Navy SEAL Team brutally killing everyone in the house. Sources further tell us that this is the latest result of an ongoing feud between two rival gangs. One gang reportedly from the Alice Griffith Housing Project, the other from right here in the Sunnydale area."

"Right now, we're being told that the police have no one in custody and do not have any suspects at this time. This is Mike Mibach Channel 2 news. Back to you, Pam."

"Uh, Mike, just a couple of quick questions." The look on Pam Cook's face made it clear she was devastated. "The six people that were found killed in that house. Do we know if all six were gang members or suspected gang members?"

"Well, Pam, we're being told that there were four male bodies and two female bodies discovered inside of the house. Now, as to the affiliation of the individuals, that is unclear. But the incident itself is suspected to be gang related. Perhaps a retaliation of several shootings that resulted in deaths in the Double Rock neighborhood earlier this week."

"My God this is all so tragic. Here at Channel 2 our hearts go out to the families of all the victims......."

Rick stopped paying attention to the rest of whatever Pam Cook was saying. He had already heard what he needed to hear. He picked his cell phone up, searched for Ebony's name and pressed send. He waited for her to answer when she did, he spoke three simple words into the phone.

"I love you."

***

"I love you too." Ebony spoke into the cell phone before hanging up.

She had been waiting on Rick's call and she fully understood the message. The timing was perfect. Because a few minutes later, she was pulling up in front of Chino's house. She parked and sent him a text message to let him know that she was there. She got out the car wearing a long tan trench coat. Underneath the coat all she had on was a tan peek-a-boo bra and G-string set. The cool, crisp, San Francisco air had her nipples fully erect under the coat. Ebony looked around, checking the area out. It was her first time at his place. She noticed a few cars on the streets with tinted windows. When her eyes landed on the all-black Monte Carlo, they lingered for a second before continuing on.

Her cell phone vibrated. She took it out of the pocket of her coat and read the text message. Chino told her that the door was open. She put the phone in her purse and walked to the front door. When she opened the door and stepped inside of the house, the first thing she saw was Chino. He was seated asshole butt naked on the living room couch stroking his hardened dick.

"Oh, so I see what's on your mind first thing in the morning." She shut the door and walked over and stood directly in front of him. "It's not going down like that though." The untied the strap to her coat and opened it revealing her flesh. "This is Mama's show." She put one foot on the couch beside him. "Taste this pussy."

Chino scooted up and leaned forward. He inhaled deeply enjoying the smell of her womanhood before devouring it with his mouth. The explosion had juices running down both sides of his chin. They switched places and Ebony sat down on the couch and Chino got on his knees and finished eating her pussy. He was slurping so loud that all he could hear were the sounds of his own mouth and Ebony's loud cries in his ears.

She was on the verge of yet another powerful, mind-blowing orgasm. She gripped the back of his head like niggaz did bitches when they were getting their dick sucked. Then she began fucking his face. She opened her eyes and held her other hand up with the index finger up, in the "hold on" position. She kept her eyes locked on the pair of eyes that was watching her. Ebony pulled Chino's head even closer. Her nutt was right there. She bucked violently. Chino clamped down on her clit and she blew.

Her fluids shot out like a geyser. The term was Gushing. which she had never done before in her life. Chino tried to swallow as much as he could, but only ending up choking on the creamy fluid. Ebony on the other hand, laid sprawled out on the couch
panting heavily.

"T-thank you, shit! A bitch needed that bad as fuck," she called out with her eyes closed and a satisfied smile on her face.

"Don't thank me for that little shit. Wait until I put this dick on you Mami." Chino replied as he still stroked his dick

"I don't think she was talking to you Puto." The sound of the voice made Chino's head snap around.

Crazy and three other Mexicans were standing in front of him. The three Mexicans all carried big ass guns. Crazy had a very shiny, very sharp machete in his hands.

"Guess you thought I was going to run away like a Pinchi Leva while you stole what don't belong to you." The look in Crazy's eyes sent chills down Chino's spine.

Fear made him break eye contact with Crazy. He turned his head around back toward Ebony. The trifling black bitch had set him up. He was ready to beat the black off her ass. The barrel of her compact 9mm pointed directly at the center of his forehead changed all those feelings. His hurt was evident, pain was written all over his face. He had begun to have feelings for Ebony. The fact that she betrayed him caused a single tear to slide down his face.

"Don't take it that way, lil' Daddy. We all follow somebody's orders. Even me." Ebony kept her gun on Chino as she swung her leg around so she could stand up. "And right now, it seems you got some shit you got to answer for, and these are the niggaz you got to answer to." She looked at Chino. No words were needed.

When Rick was doing his thing as Spank-G, Crazy was one of his young workers. He was still in school back then. Crazy was loyal and didn't take part in the scheme that his Aunties Vickie and Dee plotted. He stayed loyal. Later Spank-G would hear two voicemails that were on his phone from a young Crazy trying to warn him of what his two Aunts were up to.

Spank-G respected the level of loyalty that would have a young nigga defy the ill plans of his own flesh and blood and remain true to the bond of the group he claimed as his family. It was because of this, that he reached out to Crazy and told him about Chino's plan to take over 21st and move in a completely different direction regarding the dope game. Crazy thanked the O.G. and asked if he knew how deep the betrayal had run in his gang. Because no one knew Crazy went underground. By the end of the day an example will be made that every Norteños in Northern California would talk about for years to come, and everybody close to and loyal to Chino will be dead.

Ebony's pussy was still tingling with small aftershocks from her mighty orgasm as she got back in her car. She sent Rick a text message of a smiley face emoji and drove off.

***

The event was posted all over social media, they were giving a party in remembrance of BR. His phone had been blowing up, but he ignored every call. His body was healing nicely, but Lil' Dooka's mind and heart was fucked up. The Double Rock niggaz had managed somehow to win. Everybody that he loved, every single person that he ever called brotha or considered family, were all dead. He couldn't understand that. Shit, he himself would be dead if it wasn't for Natty. She not only saved Dooka's life, she brought new meaning to it.

Straight Beast Mode 2

In the time she spent nursing him back together, the two of them had really gotten to know each other. Natty had made Lil' Dooka feel things that he never thought he could feel. When she told him about the death of her little brother Hector, she broke down and cried. Lil' Dooka felt like a part of him was connected to Natty because he could feel every ounce of her pain. He had held her tight as she cried in his arms.

She went on to explain to Dooka how her little brother had died in her arms asking for their parents. She never went into detail about what happened. She didn't need to. He understood that her world came crashing down on her that day.
"He opened up to Natty as well, sharing with her the embarrassing hurt and pain he experienced growing up without his real biological parents. He told her that he loved his foster mom just as much as he would've loved her if she had birthed him. But that didn't stop him from having feelings and thoughts when he was a child that no one wanted or loved him.
In the weeks that they spent together Lil' Dooka found himself developing strong feelings for Natty, to the point that he was ready to say fuck Gabby and kick her to the curb. As silly as it may seem he was believing that Natty was everything a nigga could want in a wifey.
As she drove him to his apartment, these thoughts drifted through his mind. That along with the story she first told him about finding him shot up, almost dead inside of the car, when he crashed into her parents' front yard. She told him how she knew who he was from the newspaper articles and news coverage about the shooting at Tanforan Mall. Knowing she couldn't take him to the hospital, she took him to her uncle who was a vet and part time doctor for the Norteños on C-Street. At first her uncle, who was a Norteños too, didn't want to help. But once she told him who Lil' Dooka was, her uncle changed his mind and helped. He removed most of the bullets that were in him. Some went clear through. Only a couple he left because it was too dangerous to remove them. Some of the wounds had to be stitched while others just cleaned off and bandaged.

De'Kari

It was a miracle Lil' Dooka made it. He had been shot seventeen times with 9mm bullets. His recovery was even more miraculous. He would be walking inside of the celebration for BR, not laid up somewhere, weak or in some damn wheelchair looking like a weak and lame. Lil' Dooka would be walking on his own two feel like a man.

Natty pulled in front of Lil' Dooka's apartment and turned the car off. A nostalgic feeling came over him. He couldn't remember the last time he was here. But he remembered the time Chino came over to buy the E-pills, Coke and Syrup. Even Chino was dead. He'd seen that on the news last week. The past few months had been very bloody and deadly in Bayview, Hunters Point and the Visitation Valley as well as the Mission District.

"You ready, baby?" Natty leaned over and gave him a kiss of support. She knew that she couldn't understand how he felt or what was going through his mind. He shared with her about the war that was going on and all his brothas that had been killed.

"I ain't never gonna be ready Natty. This shit is killing me, but I gotta do this. I gotta show up for BR" He wiped the tears that flowed down his face. Took a deep breath and got out the car.

They walked up to the front door in silence holding hands. He took a deep breath and unlocked the door. Then they went in. It was cold as fuck inside of the apartment.

"Damn it's cold!" He blew into his hands and shivered.

"Sorry Daddy. I turned the air conditioner on high when you had me come over to get you some clothes and the other shit. I didn't want your food and shit to spoil." The only thing Lil' Dooka heard her say was Daddy. He loved when she called him Daddy. Didn't know why, but it sounded different coming from her lips.

"It's good. I'mma just turn this bitch off."

"I got it Daddy." She told him, walking over to the thermostat. "Why don't you get ready, I'mma fix you a drink and roll you a blunt so you can get right before we head over to the park."

He made his way down the hall to his room. He noticed a faint sour smell and figured her little trick didn't work too well because something had gone bad. When he opened his room door, the smell was stronger. He figured he probably left a plate of food on the nightstand. He noticed something was on his bed but couldn't make out what it was in the dark room. He turned on the lights and almost shit his pants.

It looked like somebody had wrapped a body in some plastic and left it on his bed.

"What the fuck!" He reached for his gun only to realize he didn't have one. His eyes scanned the room wondering if one of them 357 niggaz was in the room. But he didn't sense anyone else in the room. Something was left on the body where the face would be. His curiosity got the best of him. He walked over toward the bed to see what it was. It was an article cut out of the newspaper. When he picked the article up, he looked at the face and realized it was Gabby. Somebody had killed his Gabbs and left her wrapped in plastic on his bed. It was a fucked-up way to treat her. Gabby never harmed anyone. Suddenly, he felt guilty about Natty. He tried to swallow but couldn't. A tear slid down his face and hit the newspaper. He had forgotten about the article.

He turned the newspaper over and read the headline of the article that was cut from the front page. *Gang War Spills into The Public Safety of Tanforan Mall Killing Innocent Boy*. There was a photo of the scene inside of the mall. Off to the far corner a female was on her knees cradling the body of a small child.

Lil' Dooka read the article which was a follow up to the original article. This one, though it mentioned the gang background of the alleged two groups, it mainly focused on the aspect of the life that was taken.

It read:

Hector Guzman happened to be at the mall that day with his older sister who was taking him shopping for presents for his seventh birthday. Hector was carrying his first gift, a video game console, with pride as they made their way to the snack bar to get a snack before going to look for his second gift. That's when the gun shots erupted. His sister rushed them toward a store for safety. Before they could reach it, young Hector dropped the bag with his video game in it. He let go of his sister's hand and ran to pick it up. That's when two stray bullets killed young Hector. Shocked and heart broken, his older sister rushed to him with no regard for her own safety and held her baby brother in her arms as he died. Nathalie Quintanilla-Guzman said that she......

The chill that ran down his spine wasn't cold, it was artic. His breath caught in his chest, felt like ice sickles. He found it hard to breathe. He read the name again. Then again. He held the paper up close to his face for a better look at the picture. Still, he couldn't make out the face of the little bitch holding the baby.

"He was only seven years old but he was already full of big dreams and aspirations….." Lil' Dooka turned around, Natty was standing in the doorway of the room holding a Glock 27. Her face was tear stained as she spoke to him….. "He used to talk about doing good enough in school so he could go to college. He wanted to be a video game software designer. Imagine that. A seven-year-old knowing what a video game software designer was. He knew what gangs were. That shit didn't appeal to him. My little Hector said gangs were for losers. And you know what? He was right, because you losers took him away from us." She pulled the trigger.

White hot pain ripped through his stomach making him double over.

"Natty wait….." he tried to plead.

She wasn't having it. Natty fired again. This time the bullet caught him in his kneecap, shattering it. He collapsed down on the floor.

"Come on big bad ass gang banger, TIO, bitch. She fired again. "I'm gonna kill you like I did your lil' puta whore. I got here just in time to watch that cop beat and rape that little bitch right there in the front room. Once he left, I came in. She was crying like the little puta she was. I put that fat bitch out of her misery. You took something I loved from me, so I took something you loved from you. Now I will kill you for my little Mijo."

"Natty, listen... I-I'm so sorry about your little brother. I had no way of knowing. I was scared and running for my life too. It wasn't me. Them niggaz was chasing me, shooting at me. I didn't kill

Hector they did." He'd managed to pull himself back up off the ground. Natty listen, please, I told you I'm done. I don't want to be in the streets no more. Fuck gangs! Fuck TIO. I want to start a life with you. He gently hopped on one foot trying to get close to her. "Natty, I love you. You've changed me, please..." She shot again. This time the bullet flew high above his head.

It was his moment. He lunged forward and swung with all of his might. The blow caught the crazy bitch flush on her jaw. It snapped her head back. The gun flew out of her hands.

"Stupid bitch! Is you crazy mothafucka!" He punched her again. This time on the side of her head.

The energy he exhorted weakened him and caused Lil' Dooka to get lightheaded and dizzy. He fell on the bed on top of Gabby's body.

Natty saw white lights and black stars. She tried desperately to fight the cloud of unconsciousness that covered her. But it was useless. Her body dropped. She hit her head against the floorboard on the door frame knocking herself on conscious.

"Fucking stupid Mexican bitch!" Lil' Dooka spat as he raised himself off the bed.

He looked around for the gun Natty dropped. It took a minute, but he spotted it on the floor over by the closet. He was bleeding profusely. Fighting through the pain, he limped and hopped on one leg trying to make his way over to the closet. He fell once. The jolt of pain caused by the fall brought tears to his eyes.

Still, he managed to pull himself up enough to continue his pursuit. Blood was everywhere. He was losing mode blood than he realized. Finally, out of breath and sweating, he made it to the gun. When he bent down to pick it be, he became dizzy and fell over. The doors to the closet collapsed as he crashed into them. This time he remained on the ground for a moment. His body was soaked with blood and sweat. He felt around for the gun and found it.

Once he grabbed the gun, he struggled to stand up again. When he finally stood erect, he swayed back and forth fighting off another dizzy spell. Next, he hopped over to where an unconscious Natty laid on the ground.

"Bitch it's TIO for Life! I'll always be Gang-Gang! 4Ever Greezy, bitch!" He hawked up a loogey and spit it on Natty's face.

Lil' Dooka summoned all the energy he had in his body to raise his arm and aim at her head, then he pulled the trigger. He was too weak to fight the recoil. The bullet went high and slammed into the door jam. He blinked again trying to fight the dizziness. He raised his arm again and took aim. As he was squeezing the trigger everything went black.

To Be Continued…
Straight Beast 3
Coming Soon

Lock Down Publications and Ca$h Presents assisted publishing packages.

BASIC PACKAGE $499
Editing
Cover Design
Formatting

UPGRADED PACKAGE $800
Typing
Editing
Cover Design
Formatting

ADVANCE PACKAGE $1,200
Typing
Editing
Cover Design
Formatting
Copyright registration
Proofreading
Upload book to Amazon

LDP SUPREME PACKAGE $1,500
Typing
Editing
Cover Design
Formatting
Copyright registration
Proofreading
Set up Amazon account
Upload book to Amazon
Advertise on LDP Amazon and Facebook page

***Other services available upon request. Additional charges may apply
Lock Down Publications
P.O. Box 944
Stockbridge, GA 30281-9998
Phone # 470 303-9761

Submission Guideline

Submit the first three chapters of your completed manuscript to ldpsubmissions@gmail.com, subject line: Your book's title. The manuscript must be in a .doc file and sent as an attachment. Document should be in Times New Roman, double spaced and in size 12 font. Also, provide your synopsis and full contact information. If sending multiple submissions, they must each be in a separate email.

Have a story but no way to send it electronically? You can still submit to LDP/Ca$h Presents. Send in the first three chapters, written or typed, of your completed manuscript to:

LDP: Submissions Dept
Po Box 944
Stockbridge, Ga 30281

DO NOT send original manuscript. Must be a duplicate.

Provide your synopsis and a cover letter containing your full contact information.

Thanks for considering LDP and Ca$h Presents.

NEW RELEASES

THE BRICK MAN 4 by KING RIO
HOOD CONSIGLIERE by KEESE
PRETTY GIRLS DO NASTY THINGS by NICOLE GOOSBY
PROTÉGÉ OF A LEGEND by COREY ROBINSON
STRAIGHT BEAST MODE 2 by DE'KARI

Coming Soon from Lock Down Publications/Ca$h Presents
BLOOD OF A BOSS **VI**
SHADOWS OF THE GAME II
TRAP BASTARD II
By **Askari**
LOYAL TO THE GAME **IV**
By **T.J. & Jelissa**
IF TRUE SAVAGE **VIII**
MIDNIGHT CARTEL IV
DOPE BOY MAGIC IV
CITY OF KINGZ III
NIGHTMARE ON SILENT AVE II
THE PLUG OF LIL MEXICO II
By **Chris Green**
BLAST FOR ME **III**
A SAVAGE DOPEBOY III
CUTTHROAT MAFIA III
DUFFLE BAG CARTEL VII
HEARTLESS GOON VI
By **Ghost**
A HUSTLER'S DECEIT III
KILL ZONE II
BAE BELONGS TO ME III
By **Aryanna**
KING OF THE TRAP III
By **T.J. Edwards**
GORILLAZ IN THE BAY V
3X KRAZY III
STRAIGHT BEAST MODE III
De'Kari

De'Kari

KINGPIN KILLAZ IV
STREET KINGS III
PAID IN BLOOD III
CARTEL KILLAZ IV
DOPE GODS III
Hood Rich
SINS OF A HUSTLA II
ASAD
RICH $AVAGE II
By Martell Troublesome Bolden
YAYO V
Bred In The Game 2
S. Allen
CREAM III
THE STREETS WILL TALK II
By Yolanda Moore
SON OF A DOPE FIEND III
HEAVEN GOT A GHETTO II
By Renta
LOYALTY AIN'T PROMISED III
By Keith Williams
I'M NOTHING WITHOUT HIS LOVE II
SINS OF A THUG II
TO THE THUG I LOVED BEFORE II
IN A HUSTLER I TRUST II
By Monet Dragun
QUIET MONEY IV
EXTENDED CLIP III
THUG LIFE IV
By **Trai'Quan**

Straight Beast Mode 2

THE STREETS MADE ME IV
By **Larry D. Wright**
IF YOU CROSS ME ONCE II
By **Anthony Fields**
THE STREETS WILL NEVER CLOSE IV
By K'ajji
HARD AND RUTHLESS III
KILLA KOUNTY III
By Khufu
MONEY GAME III
By Smoove Dolla
JACK BOYS VS DOPE BOYS II
A GANGSTA'S QUR'AN V
COKE GIRLZ II
By Romell Tukes
MURDA WAS THE CASE II
Elijah R. Freeman
THE STREETS NEVER LET GO II
By Robert Baptiste
AN UNFORESEEN LOVE III
By **Meesha**
KING OF THE TRENCHES III
by **GHOST & TRANAY ADAMS**

MONEY MAFIA II
LOYAL TO THE SOIL III
By **Jibril Williams**
QUEEN OF THE ZOO II
By **Black Migo**
VICIOUS LOYALTY III
By Kingpen

De'Kari

A GANGSTA'S PAIN III
By J-Blunt
CONFESSIONS OF A JACKBOY III
By Nicholas Lock
GRIMEY WAYS II
By Ray Vinci
KING KILLA II
By Vincent "Vitto" Holloway
BETRAYAL OF A THUG II
By Fre$h
THE MURDER QUEENS II
By Michael Gallon
THE BIRTH OF A GANGSTER II
By Delmont Player
TREAL LOVE II
By Le'Monica Jackson
FOR THE LOVE OF BLOOD II
By Jamel Mitchell
RAN OFF ON DA PLUG II
By Paper Boi Rari
HOOD CONSIGLIERE II
By Keese
PRETTY GIRLS DO NASTY THINGS II
By Nicole Goosby
PROTÉGÉ OF A LEGEND II
By Corey Robinson

Straight Beast Mode 2

Available Now

RESTRAINING ORDER **I & II**
By **CA$H & Coffee**
LOVE KNOWS NO BOUNDARIES **I II & III**
By **Coffee**
RAISED AS A GOON I, II, III & IV
BRED BY THE SLUMS I, II, III
BLAST FOR ME I & II
ROTTEN TO THE CORE I II III
A BRONX TALE I, II, III
DUFFLE BAG CARTEL I II III IV V VI
HEARTLESS GOON I II III IV V
A SAVAGE DOPEBOY I II
DRUG LORDS I II III
CUTTHROAT MAFIA I II
KING OF THE TRENCHES
By **Ghost**
LAY IT DOWN **I & II**
LAST OF A DYING BREED I II
BLOOD STAINS OF A SHOTTA I & II III
By **Jamaica**
LOYAL TO THE GAME I II III
LIFE OF SIN I, II III
By **TJ & Jelissa**
BLOODY COMMAS I & II
SKI MASK CARTEL I II & III
KING OF NEW YORK I II,III IV V
RISE TO POWER I II III
COKE KINGS I II III IV V

De'Kari

BORN HEARTLESS I II III IV
KING OF THE TRAP I II
By **T.J. Edwards**
IF LOVING HIM IS WRONG...I & II
LOVE ME EVEN WHEN IT HURTS I II III
By **Jelissa**
WHEN THE STREETS CLAP BACK I & II III
THE HEART OF A SAVAGE I II III
MONEY MAFIA
LOYAL TO THE SOIL I II
By **Jibril Williams**
A DISTINGUISHED THUG STOLE MY HEART I II & III
LOVE SHOULDN'T HURT I II III IV
RENEGADE BOYS I II III IV
PAID IN KARMA I II III
SAVAGE STORMS I II III
AN UNFORESEEN LOVE I II
By **Meesha**
A GANGSTER'S CODE I &, II III
A GANGSTER'S SYN I II III
THE SAVAGE LIFE I II III
CHAINED TO THE STREETS I II III
BLOOD ON THE MONEY I II III
A GANGSTA'S PAIN I II
By J-Blunt
PUSH IT TO THE LIMIT
By **Bre' Hayes**
BLOOD OF A BOSS **I, II, III, IV, V**
SHADOWS OF THE GAME
TRAP BASTARD

By **Askari**
THE STREETS BLEED MURDER **I, II & III**
THE HEART OF A GANGSTA I II& III
By **Jerry Jackson**
CUM FOR ME I II III IV V VI VII VIII
An **LDP Erotica Collaboration**
BRIDE OF A HUSTLA **I II & II**
THE FETTI GIRLS **I, II& III**
CORRUPTED BY A GANGSTA I, II III, IV
BLINDED BY HIS LOVE
THE PRICE YOU PAY FOR LOVE I, II ,III
DOPE GIRL MAGIC I II III
By **Destiny Skai**
WHEN A GOOD GIRL GOES BAD
By **Adrienne**
THE COST OF LOYALTY I II III
By Kweli
A GANGSTER'S REVENGE **I II III & IV**
THE BOSS MAN'S DAUGHTERS I II III IV V
A SAVAGE LOVE **I & II**
BAE BELONGS TO ME I II
A HUSTLER'S DECEIT I, II, III
WHAT BAD BITCHES DO I, II, III
SOUL OF A MONSTER I II III
KILL ZONE
A DOPE BOY'S QUEEN I II III
By **Aryanna**
A KINGPIN'S AMBITON
A KINGPIN'S AMBITION **II**
I MURDER FOR THE DOUGH

De'Kari

By **Ambitious**
TRUE SAVAGE I II III IV V VI VII
DOPE BOY MAGIC I, II, III
MIDNIGHT CARTEL I II III
CITY OF KINGZ I II
NIGHTMARE ON SILENT AVE
THE PLUG OF LIL MEXICO II

By **Chris Green**
A DOPEBOY'S PRAYER
By **Eddie "Wolf" Lee**
THE KING CARTEL **I, II & III**
By **Frank Gresham**
THESE NIGGAS AIN'T LOYAL **I, II & III**
By **Nikki Tee**
GANGSTA SHYT **I II &III**
By **CATO**
THE ULTIMATE BETRAYAL
By **Phoenix**
BOSS'N UP **I , II & III**
By **Royal Nicole**
I LOVE YOU TO DEATH
By **Destiny J**
I RIDE FOR MY HITTA
I STILL RIDE FOR MY HITTA
By **Misty Holt**
LOVE & CHASIN' PAPER
By **Qay Crockett**
TO DIE IN VAIN
SINS OF A HUSTLA

Straight Beast Mode 2

By **ASAD**
BROOKLYN HUSTLAZ
By **Boogsy Morina**
BROOKLYN ON LOCK I & II
By **Sonovia**
GANGSTA CITY
By **Teddy Duke**
A DRUG KING AND HIS DIAMOND I & II III
A DOPEMAN'S RICHES
HER MAN, MINE'S TOO I, II
CASH MONEY HO'S
THE WIFEY I USED TO BE I II
PRETTY GIRLS DO NASTY THINGS
By Nicole Goosby
TRAPHOUSE KING **I II & III**
KINGPIN KILLAZ I II III
STREET KINGS I II
PAID IN BLOOD **I II**
CARTEL KILLAZ I II III
DOPE GODS I II
By **Hood Rich**
LIPSTICK KILLAH **I, II, III**
CRIME OF PASSION I II & III
FRIEND OR FOE I II III
By **Mimi**
STEADY MOBBN' **I, II, III**
THE STREETS STAINED MY SOUL I II III
By **Marcellus Allen**
WHO SHOT YA **I, II, III**
SON OF A DOPE FIEND I II

De'Kari

HEAVEN GOT A GHETTO
Renta
GORILLAZ IN THE BAY **I II III IV**
TEARS OF A GANGSTA I II
3X KRAZY I II
STRAIGHT BEAST MODE I II
DE'KARI
TRIGGADALE I II III
MURDAROBER WAS THE CASE
Elijah R. Freeman
GOD BLESS THE TRAPPERS I, II, III
THESE SCANDALOUS STREETS I, II, III
FEAR MY GANGSTA I, II, III IV, V
THESE STREETS DON'T LOVE NOBODY I, II
BURY ME A G I, II, III, IV, V
A GANGSTA'S EMPIRE I, II, III, IV
THE DOPEMAN'S BODYGAURD I II
THE REALEST KILLAZ I II III
THE LAST OF THE OGS I II III
Tranay Adams
THE STREETS ARE CALLING
Duquie Wilson
MARRIED TO A BOSS I II III
By Destiny Skai & Chris Green
KINGZ OF THE GAME I II III IV V VI
Playa Ray
SLAUGHTER GANG I II III
RUTHLESS HEART I II III
By Willie Slaughter
FUK SHYT

Straight Beast Mode 2

By Blakk Diamond
DON'T F#CK WITH MY HEART I II
By Linnea
ADDICTED TO THE DRAMA I II III
IN THE ARM OF HIS BOSS II
By Jamila
YAYO I II III IV
A SHOOTER'S AMBITION I II
BRED IN THE GAME
By S. Allen
TRAP GOD I II III
RICH $AVAGE
MONEY IN THE GRAVE I II III
By Martell Troublesome Bolden
FOREVER GANGSTA
GLOCKS ON SATIN SHEETS I II
By Adrian Dulan
TOE TAGZ I II III IV
LEVELS TO THIS SHYT I II
By Ah'Million
KINGPIN DREAMS I II III
RAN OFF ON DA PLUG
By Paper Boi Rari
CONFESSIONS OF A GANGSTA I II III IV
CONFESSIONS OF A JACKBOY I II
By Nicholas Lock
I'M NOTHING WITHOUT HIS LOVE
SINS OF A THUG
TO THE THUG I LOVED BEFORE
A GANGSTA SAVED XMAS

De'Kari

IN A HUSTLER I TRUST
By Monet Dragun
CAUGHT UP IN THE LIFE I II III
THE STREETS NEVER LET GO
By Robert Baptiste
NEW TO THE GAME I II III
MONEY, MURDER & MEMORIES I II III
By **Malik D. Rice**
LIFE OF A SAVAGE I II III
A GANGSTA'S QUR'AN I II III IV
MURDA SEASON I II III
GANGLAND CARTEL I II III
CHI'RAQ GANGSTAS I II III
KILLERS ON ELM STREET I II III
JACK BOYZ N DA BRONX I II III
A DOPEBOY'S DREAM I II III
JACK BOYS VS DOPE BOYS
COKE GIRLZ
By Romell Tukes
LOYALTY AIN'T PROMISED I II
By Keith Williams
QUIET MONEY I II III
THUG LIFE I II III
EXTENDED CLIP I II
By **Trai'Quan**
THE STREETS MADE ME I II III
By **Larry D. Wright**
THE ULTIMATE SACRIFICE I, II, III, IV, V, VI
KHADIFI
IF YOU CROSS ME ONCE

223

Straight Beast Mode 2

ANGEL I II
IN THE BLINK OF AN EYE
By **Anthony Fields**
THE LIFE OF A HOOD STAR
By **Ca$h & Rashia Wilson**
THE STREETS WILL NEVER CLOSE I II III
By **K'ajji**
CREAM I II
THE STREETS WILL TALK
By **Yolanda Moore**
NIGHTMARES OF A HUSTLA I II III
By **King Dream**
CONCRETE KILLA I II III
VICIOUS LOYALTY I II
By **Kingpen**
HARD AND RUTHLESS I II
MOB TOWN 251
THE BILLIONAIRE BENTLEYS I II III
By **Von Diesel**
GHOST MOB
Stilloan Robinson
MOB TIES I II III IV V VI
By **SayNoMore**
BODYMORE MURDERLAND I II III
THE BIRTH OF A GANGSTER
By **Delmont Player**
FOR THE LOVE OF A BOSS
By **C. D. Blue**
MOBBED UP I II III IV
THE BRICK MAN I II III IV

De'Kari

THE COCAINE PRINCESS I II III IV V
By King Rio
KILLA KOUNTY I II III
By Khufu
MONEY GAME I II
By Smoove Dolla
A GANGSTA'S KARMA I II
By FLAME
KING OF THE TRENCHES I II
by **GHOST & TRANAY ADAMS**
QUEEN OF THE ZOO
By **Black Migo**
GRIMEY WAYS
By Ray Vinci
XMAS WITH AN ATL SHOOTER
By Ca$h & Destiny Skai
KING KILLA
By Vincent "Vitto" Holloway
BETRAYAL OF A THUG
By Fre$h
THE MURDER QUEENS
By Michael Gallon
TREAL LOVE
By Le'Monica Jackson
FOR THE LOVE OF BLOOD
By Jamel Mitchell
HOOD CONSIGLIERE
By Keese
PROTÉGÉ OF A LEGEND
By Corey Robinson

Straight Beast Mode 2

BOOKS BY LDP'S CEO, CA$H

TRUST IN NO MAN
TRUST IN NO MAN 2
TRUST IN NO MAN 3
BONDED BY BLOOD
SHORTY GOT A THUG
THUGS CRY
THUGS CRY 2
THUGS CRY 3
TRUST NO BITCH
TRUST NO BITCH 2
TRUST NO BITCH 3
TIL MY CASKET DROPS
RESTRAINING ORDER
RESTRAINING ORDER 2
IN LOVE WITH A CONVICT
LIFE OF A HOOD STAR
XMAS WITH AN ATL SHOOTER

De'Kari

CPSIA information can be obtained
at www.ICGtesting.com
Printed in the USA
LVHW012200140822
725931LV00002B/226